S.M. LEVINE

Couples Session

First edition

ISBN: 979-8-9919826-3-4

This book was professionally typeset on Reedsy.
Find out more at reedsy.com

For my family

Contents

Preface

Dear Reader,

Thank you so much for choosing my book! Vanessa and Noah's story is the second book in The Well Space series, and while it can be read as a standalone, the books work best when read in order.

Vanessa is a couples counselor who's bad at love. She loves love, but it doesn't always love her back. Through reconnecting with her ex-boyfriend Noah, she discovers a lot of important truths about herself along the way. And the most important one is this: to trust that she can and will be held up by the person she loves.

Noah's great at appliance repair, but not so great at having conversations—or dealing with family crises. He's lucky Vanessa is so good at communication, because the more he opens up to her, the more he's able to see solutions to his family problems he never could have predicted.

Couples Session is an open-door contemporary romance. Tropes include: Second chance, snowed in, forced proximity, and fake not-dating, which is when you pretend you're not dating, but you actually are. Trigger warnings for the book include: Verbal abuse (off page), abandonment by a parent, alcohol consumption, and divorce. If this content might be triggering for you, please take care and consider if reading this book is right for you.

I had such a great time writing these characters, and I hope you enjoy their story!

Happy reading,

S.M. Levine

Introduction

Snowed in with her ex ... and one more chance to work it out.

Couples counselor Vanessa never met a relationship problem she couldn't solve—except for her own recent breakup. She'd been so sure Noah was the one, but after he ghosted her without an explanation, she's completely moved on. She's even starting a new relationships podcast, so she can help others avoid her mistakes. But a snowstorm leaves her stranded at work the night before Valentine's Day, and the last person she wants to see shows up to tow her car.

Noah Green is the king of awkward conversation. After a lifetime of putting his foot in his mouth, he mostly stays quiet and works with his hands, managing his family's appliance repair shop. He'd never really opened up to anyone before, until he met the woman of his dreams—and then lost her a few months later. If Vanessa knew about the family problems that made him break up with her, she'd never want him back anyway.

When Noah crashes his truck in the clinic parking lot,

forcing them to spend the night there together, their scorching chemistry reignites by morning. A fragile truce leads them to try dating again, all while pretending to be just friends around Noah's broken family. But family problems are harder to fix than appliances, and in the meantime, their fake not-dating starts to feel a lot like the real thing ...

Chapter 1

The couple arguing in Vanessa's earbuds escalated in volume, and she put down her pen to lower the sound on her phone. She'd recorded her former clients' session with the couple's permission, but the voices on the playback sounded a lot louder than she remembered them being in person. Maybe having their voices right in her ears made it worse.

"I'm not saying you're thinking about other women," Emily said, her voice carrying an edge of discomfort.

The older woman, who always looked calm and put together in high-end athleisure sets, had been pink in the face. Normally, she deflected her husband Ron's teasing with a forced smile. It didn't help that he never gave her a straight answer.

"So if you're not saying it, don't say it," he replied, his tone even.

"Well, what if I was saying it?" A beat of silence met Emily's light question before Ron answered.

"Look, babe. Every time I speak to a woman who's not you,

this comes up."

"Have you ever thought there might be something in how you speak to them?"

"This is what you want to talk about? When we have so many other things we could discuss?"

The sudden sharp edge to Ron's voice sent a shiver down Vanessa's spine, and she hit the pause button on the playback. The conversation had gotten really intense for about three minutes. Then Ron had shut it down, returning to his usual smiles, deflecting, and teasing. They'd been so close to the heart of one of their major problems.

Moments like that, when couples teetered on the edge of a breakthrough, were what kept her going. The sudden lightbulb of understanding, the hint of real change about to happen—it sent a thrill up her spine every time.

She'd worked a dozen extra hours this week, prepping for her upcoming podcast taping. The new show was so close to being ready to launch. She had all the equipment ready—the podcast microphone set up, recording and editing software installed on her laptop. She'd taken notes on dozens of client sessions, looking for threads to draw out in the show.

This could be how she left her mark on the clinic. She'd reach hundreds more people who might need help, outside of her own client workload.

Too bad there was no helping her own relationship issues.

She tapped her pencil on the edge of her notebook, then tossed it down, restless. It was the night before Valentine's Day, her former favorite holiday, and she'd worked late again. Partly because she loved her work, and partly to avoid her empty apartment and the memories of last year's Valentine's Day. Last year, when she'd been happily paired up with a man

4

who finally, finally seemed to be the one.

Until he wasn't. Just like every other guy before him. He'd ghosted her without any explanation, which meant one thing in her experience. He'd met someone else.

"Red flags," she muttered under her breath. "I specialize in red flags."

Still, she hadn't seen this one coming. Noah had been perfect—attentive, kind, a hell of a cook, and up for any adventure in bed. Their three months together had started to mean something to her. But they hadn't meant as much to him.

He'd stopped texting her back, stopped answering her calls, and the hurt had been so sharp, she'd struggled to put it in perspective. Every relationship she'd been in had ended, so she shouldn't have been surprised this one had, too. Things always went well for a while, until the first hint of a red flag appeared on the horizon and it was time to call it quits.

The least she could do was try to help other people avoid her mistakes. It wasn't as satisfying as coming home to Noah's homemade dinners and warm hugs, but it wasn't nothing, either. And she wouldn't think of him tonight, anyway, because he didn't deserve to take up any more space in her brain. She was thriving, contributing to her field in a meaningful way. And also, she was alone.

With a sigh, she reached for the playback button, about to continue her note-taking. A knock on her office door stopped her hand mid-air.

She pulled out her earbud and found her co-worker Cameron standing at the door frame. The younger man's black, curly hair was a mess, standing up in all directions, and dark circles ringed his eyes.

"What are you doing here this late?" She leaned back in her chair, studying him.

"Just working on some stuff for school. Better internet speed here." He shoved a hand through his hair, making it stand up even taller. His grad school coursework, which he completed in the off hours he wasn't working as an admin assistant at the clinic, seemed to take more out of him every day.

"You need this time off," she told him. "Therefore, you shouldn't be here. This week will be good for you."

He groaned. "It will not be good for me. I can't believe Ben is making me take my vacation days."

"His rules, not mine." A grin spread across her face as she remembered Ben's stern reminder email to the staff about employees being forced to take all their paid time off every year. For her, it wasn't a problem. But for a workaholic like Cameron, it was torture.

She and Ben had co-founded The Well Space clinic ten years ago, and up until this year, he'd been pretty much the most grumpy, closed-off man she'd ever met. Then he'd met the love of his life, gotten happier, and decided everyone at the clinic needed to take better care of themselves.

"You could use some time away from this place," she added, eying Cameron's wrinkled dress shirt.

The younger man scrubbed a hand over his face. "Yeah. So then when I come back, I'll have twice as much to take care of in half the time."

"Let that be a problem for future Cameron. Present Cameron needs a hot meal. And twelve hours of sleep."

He snorted a laugh. "I'm lucky if I get four. But okay. I'm out of here."

He straightened from where he'd been leaning on the door

frame, squaring his shoulders. He always wore suspenders, and sometimes a matching bow tie, over his work button-downs. Today's suspenders were patterned with different species of moths.

"And what are *you* doing here this late?" he asked, squinting at her. "I should have asked you the same thing you asked me."

She gestured to the notebook in front of her, half-full with pink scrawling ink. "Taking notes. Trying to get this podcast off the ground in the next two weeks."

"Ah. The top secret plan." He nodded knowingly.

She shifted in her chair, uncomfortable. "It's not a secret. I just didn't want to bother Ben with it until he's back from his honeymoon."

Which was in two weeks, which would give her enough time to get this project started before he got here. It wasn't a secret, but also, she did want to have a complete product to show him when he got back, rather than a half-baked idea. That way, he'd be less likely to say not to bother with it.

It was a far-fetched idea, giving relationship advice to strangers. Maybe a little too trendy for her reserved partner's approval.

Cameron slung his laptop bag across his shoulder. "Well, you don't have to worry about me saying anything to him. Because I'm being forced out of here."

"That's right. Out with you." She shooed him away with her hands, silver bracelets clicking together on her wrists.

"Going." He bobbed his head. "You'd better go soon, too. The forecast said this freezing rain would make the roads pretty bad tonight."

"Yeah, I heard." Something like that had caught her attention earlier as she'd scanned her news app. She had four-wheel drive on her mini-SUV. She'd make the ten-minute drive home fine.

"All right. G'night, then," he said.

"Good night, Cameron."

She watched his lanky frame disappear down the hallway, then turned and hit play on the argument again.

This podcast could be a game-changer for the clinic if it went off well. But the research had to be spotless. Perfect notes, great examples, on-point advice. And of course, stellar interview sessions. Not like a counseling session on air. More like a comforting conversation with another couple who'd been through some of the same things her listeners might be experiencing. Advice and community.

The Well Space was known for trying cutting-edge therapy techniques, and with a podcast, she could deliver content in a new way. Ben had put the clinic on the map by writing a series of bestselling books, and she could solidify their place at the top of the pack with a stellar podcast showcasing the value of couples therapy. Ben might laugh at her, or tell her this podcast was a terrible idea when he got back in two weeks. But he might say yes if he saw how well her plan worked in action.

This was her work, her purpose—helping people find their way to healthier relationships. This was the way she'd pay it forward and reach more people.

If she could help one person avoid making her own mistakes … She flipped the page over in her notebook with a sharp snap. Her personal mistakes would fill an entire season of a podcast. A stack of notebooks. In her thirty-five years, she'd accumulated a lifetime of unfortunate experiences.

Not that she'd be sharing any of those particular details with her listeners. This was about their needs, not hers.

And if her own love life was a tangled mess, that was for her to sort through alone. So what if it was the night before Valentine's Day, and she hadn't even tried to find a date. Dates had gotten a lot less interesting in the last year.

An hour and a half later, she'd listened to two more recorded couples therapy sessions, she had another dozen pages of notes scribbled down in her admittedly illegible handwriting, and it was after 10:00 p.m.

She closed the notebook and clicked off the heart-shaped lamp on her desk. Stretching her arms overhead, she regarded her office, decorated in shades of pink, red, and white, from the fuschia couch to the pink velvet wingback desk chair. Maybe she'd overdone the pink-and-red theme with the heart-shaped fairy lights and the cherry silk curtains.

But she loved love. Even if it didn't always love her back.

She drew on her vintage tweed coat—a massive find from an estate sale—and loaded her laptop into her leather backpack. In case the weather was too bad to come into work tomorrow.

She shut off the office lights and made her way to the clinic's front door. The floorboards creaked under her heeled boots, echoing to the high ceilings of the quirky old Victorian house that held the clinic.

Ten years ago, she'd been put in charge of finding furniture for the space, and she'd scoured Kansas City's flea markets and estate sales for the antique roll-top desks, floral throw rugs, and stained glass lamps accenting the rooms. She'd outdone herself. Stepping into the clinic felt like stepping back in time, into a cozy-old fashioned hug of a space.

But the front door weighed a ton, and as she pulled at the iron handle with her full weight to wrench it open, two things hit her at once. One, the door had frozen shut. And two, it was snowing outside.

And not a little bit of snow. A blizzard of swirling snow so thick, she could barely see her car from the front door.

"This is what you get for working late, Bernhard," she muttered under her breath. "Also, great job not checking the weather forecast all afternoon. Nicely done."

She managed to get the alarm set and the door shut and locked behind her. Her stomach dropped a fraction at her first step off the wraparound porch, though, when her two-inch heel disappeared all the way into the snow.

"Shit." Her heel slipped out from under her, and she caught her balance at the last minute.

Underneath the snow was a sheet of ice, from the earlier freezing rain. Her pulse picked up, because this was not great weather for driving, even though she lived close by. She could slide off the road in a second on a surface this slick. Still, the main roads had to have been plowed by now.

Her car door had frozen shut, too. She hurled her body weight backward to pry it open, slid inside, and started the engine. With the defroster on, she pulled out her ice scraper from the back seat. The tiny plastic blade with a pink rubber handle looked woefully inadequate.

Outside the car, she scraped two decent-sized holes into the ice on her windshield, then went to the back of the car and cleared another small spot. It would be like driving through binoculars, but she could make it home this way.

"Not smart. Very not smart," she grumbled as she launched herself back into the car and threw the stupid, toy-sized ice scraper onto the seat next to her.

She should be better prepared for an emergency situation.

Chapter 1

Which this was not. Not an emergency at all. But once again, she'd chosen the pretty thing over the useful one, which was the kind of thing that had always gotten her in trouble. With clothes, with men.

She put the car in reverse and touched the gas pedal with the pointed toe of her boot. The car's tires spun in place for a second before lurching her backward out of the parking spot.

She had one second of feeling in control of the car before it slid sideways, a direction the tires didn't normally go. She shrieked, and her hands released their death grip on the wheel to cover her face. Free of any controlling force, the steering wheel spun, and the car did a slow one-eighty.

It slid to a stop when the driver's side door thudded against a lamp post, leaving the back left tire hanging off the edge of the pavement. The car hung at a diagonal angle, tilting downward on the steep, grassy slope leading to the drainage ditch.

She took a shuddering inhale and removed her hands from her face.

"It's okay. I'm okay. That's what a crash going at five miles an hour feels like. Things could have been worse."

Positive self-talk. Not an emergency. She pressed a hand to her chest, where her heart thundered.

She wasn't going to be able to open her driver's side door and exit the car, and she couldn't drive the car out of its current position either, halfway on the wet grass. This was a tow truck situation. She'd make a call, and someone would show up to help. She pulled her cell phone from her bag with a shaking hand.

A half hour and five phone calls later, she dropped the phone into her lap. Of course every tow truck in the city was unavailable right now. The shortest wait time she'd been quoted—if they'd even bothered to answer at all—was over three hours.

"Okay." She drew in a shaky breath. "Couch it is."

She'd spent the night on her office couch before, and it looked like she'd be doing it again tonight. At the very least, she'd be waiting in the clinic until the early hours of the morning. Which was no problem. No problem at all.

Except tomorrow was Valentine's Day. And she was here, at work. With nothing but her notebooks, and her clients' arguments, and her office full of hearts. She drew in a shaky breath, because she was alone in this situation.

She'd been alone a lot of her life, but sometimes, it would be really nice to have someone to call.

She wouldn't think about Noah again. The man who she'd thought she could love this time, for the long haul. That was the way it always went, with her heart. Start to trust and open up, then the red flag appeared out of nowhere.

Noah had a tow hitch on his truck, which he used to haul a trailer for his appliance repair business. But she wouldn't be calling him, because he wasn't hers to call, and hadn't been for ten months. His face should not appear in her mind at this moment, or the memory of his strong arms, or the comforting smell of detergent on his flannel shirt.

Memories always reared their stupid, inconvenient heads at the worst time. She blinked, gathered her things out of the front seat, and prepared to exit the passenger door.

Her brain didn't register the light sweeping the parking lot at first, or what it meant, because she was too busy crawling across the front seat. When the light blinded her, she dropped back into the driver's seat with a thud.

A pickup truck, much higher off the ground than her car,

swung into the lot and faced her head-on. The beams of the headlights caught thick bands of snow, and she put up a hand to shield her eyes.

This could not possibly be what she thought it was, what her over-active imagination was telling her.

The truck door swung open and a man stepped out of it, slammed the door, and took a few steps in her direction. His broad shape was silhouetted against the light, hard to make out, but he had the right height and build. The way he moved was familiar, too, steady and purposeful.

"Noah." The name came out on a puff of frozen air as he crunched through the snow toward her car.

He stopped when he got to the passenger-side door. Now that he was no longer backlit by the headlights, his face was clear in the dim yellow light of the street lamp. A square, serious face, with pale skin and brown eyes, brown beard trimmed short, and a blue beanie pulled low on his forehead. He wore a canvas work coat, jeans, and work boots, and nothing had ever looked better on anyone.

"Vanessa? You in there? Can you hear me?"

His voice didn't sound as calm and soothing as she remembered it being. Maybe he thought she was injured. Maybe he'd only raised his voice to be heard over the wind, which whipped snowflakes around him with vicious fury.

She gripped the steering wheel and tried not to laugh at the situation. Any other man on the planet could have come to help her out, and she'd have been flooded with relief at this moment. But not this man. The one person she didn't need to see was the one who'd shown up. Exactly in line with her luck with men.

She set her jaw. She was still mad at him. She would not give him anything out of this exchange. He got zero more ounces of her energy or attention.

He'd fucking *ghosted* her, then sent her a six-word reply after two weeks of silence, and who even did that to someone they'd come to care about as a human being? So he'd met someone else, didn't want to be tied down, and was trying to let her down easy. At the least, he could have said so.

And now he'd shown up here in the middle of the night, in the middle of a snowstorm, which made even less sense. Maybe he'd just been driving by. Maybe he thought he could rescue her as some sort of pathetic way of saying he was sorry.

She might need help, but she wouldn't ask him for it. She didn't have to make this easy for him. Drawing in a deep breath, she squared her shoulders and lifted her chin.

She pressed the button to roll down the passenger-side window and fixed him with her most neutral, guarded therapist expression. The one she'd give her most difficult patients when they tried to get past her defenses and dig into her emotions.

"Noah. What are you doing here?" she asked, keeping her tone as light as if they'd run into each other at a coffee shop.

She had the satisfaction of seeing his mouth open, then snap shut. He stared at her, not answering for a full minute. Then he shut his eyes, shook his head, and stomped back to his truck.

Chapter 2

Noah's boots sank ankle-deep into the snow as he trudged to the bed of his pickup to get a shovel. The muffled crunch of his steps was a lot slower than his heart rate, which had sped into overdrive at the sight of Vanessa's red, toy-sized SUV hanging halfway into the ditch. His heart hadn't slowed when she'd rolled down her window and looked at him with that steady gaze, her green eyes cool and distant. As if he was a stranger.

The sight of her face, pale with shock and cold, even as she tried to act nonchalant, hadn't helped calm him down at all. She was scared, and there was nothing he could say or do, because she clearly didn't want his help.

It was no less than he deserved. He deserved worse, in fact. Which was why he'd stayed away from her the last few months. Maybe some part of him hoped that with no contact, they'd both feel better. She'd go on with her life, and he'd deal with the disaster that had become his.

But Valentine's Day meant something to her. The last few

weeks, he'd felt the date approach, and turned over this crazy idea in his mind. He could drop by and leave her something, a note or a card. He'd shot down his own idea a dozen times, because he was not good with words, so what the hell would he write in a card?

The idea hadn't left, though, and like a teenager getting ready for a school dance, he'd gone and bought flowers today. A bouquet of overpriced pink roses, half-frozen already on the front seat of his truck. Roses were finicky, and so were relationships. Both were a lot harder to fix than washing machines and refrigerators.

He'd planned to drop the flowers on her apartment porch and leave. To let her know he'd thought of her, not to try to talk to her. Then the weather had acted up, and he'd spent the first part of the evening towing two of his neighbors out of their parking spots. He'd been on his way to Vanessa's apartment, passed by her clinic, and seen the flash of red, half in and half out of the street lamp's shadow.

His heart had stopped for a second before doing a hard reboot. This was not okay, had been his first thought. She was at work alone, late at night, for one thing. And no one had helped her. Even though she hated accepting help, she needed it sometimes.

Story of his life. People needing help and not taking it. Cleaning up messes. Still, he had to be so careful to keep the mess of his personal life from touching her.

Shovel in hand, he climbed into the truck cab, executed a careful three-point turn in the parking lot, and pulled the truck in front of her, aligning the back bumper with her front bumper. He'd dig out her tires, get her unstuck, and get gone. And hope she never found out he'd been stupid enough to buy those flowers.

Leaving the engine running, he got out of the truck and shoveled around her tires while she watched him through the windshield. He tossed the shovel aside and knelt in front of her car, securing the nylon recovery strap to the tow hook under her front bumper.

Her window rolled down again as he worked, and she draped her elbow over the side, observing him in silence. She looked calm, like she was getting ready to order food from a drive-through, rather than get towed in the middle of a blizzard. After a few minutes of watching him, she spoke.

"You don't have to do that. I'm fine."

She wasn't fine. But it wasn't the time to say that. He grunted and continued the process of securing her car, testing the connections with a hard tug before standing and brushing his gloves off on his jeans.

He did not look at her, because looking at her made his heart rate kick up and his chest feel hot, the way it did when he ate too much of Silvia's salsa verde. Heartburn was the worst.

"Noah. I didn't ask you to help. I was heading inside to wait for the tow truck I called for myself." A hint of impatience colored the words.

"And when were they coming by?" He studied his boots.

She hesitated a beat. "Three hours."

"Okay. You wanna wait three hours?"

"I ... No, not really."

"Okay. I'll get you out of here, then. You should've steered left when you started to skid. Put the car in neutral before I start to move the truck."

He turned his back on her, but hadn't taken a step yet when she called after him.

17

"Wait! Why left? The car was swerving to the left."

He turned to face her, and luckily couldn't see her very well with the light reflecting off her windshield.

"You steer into a skid when you start to slide. It doesn't look like you did that."

"I couldn't. My hands were too busy covering my eyes."

"Covering …" Noah shut his own eyes for a moment before opening them. This woman was the smartest person he'd ever met, but she'd also once asked him what a Phillips screwdriver was. Now was not the time to bring that up.

He settled for, "You could've been hurt."

She swallowed. "I know."

"Don't take your hands off the wheel when you drive." Now the image of her spinning out of control, hands over her eyes, was burned into his brain. He took a steadying breath and stomped back to the cab.

The Well Space parking lot was tiny, without a lot of room to maneuver the length of the truck plus the SUV. On a good-weather day, it would be tricky. And tonight was a mess.

The first tap of his accelerator moved the truck zero inches forward. The tires spun on the ice layer under the snow.

Cursing under his breath, he turned the steering wheel left and right, alternating with taps of the accelerator until the truck moved forward an inch. At the first hint of motion, he gave it a bit more gas, what would have been a cautious amount on a normal day.

The truck jerked forward, and the combined weight of the two vehicles added momentum to the movement on the icy surface. They flew out of the parking space, across the lot, and skidded sideways into the snowbank, where the city plow had heaped up three feet of fallen snow on the side of the road.

Behind him, Vanessa's terrified shriek carried from her open window as they ground to a halt. He threw the truck into park and launched himself across the bench seat and out the passenger door.

She'd covered her eyes again, hands clamped to her face and shoulders shaking with tension.

"I'm sorry—"

"Don't." She cut him off with the sharp word. "I need a minute. Just give me a minute."

Her chest rose and fell with a couple of deep breaths, before she removed her hands from her face and looked up at him, and oh, God, he hadn't been standing this close to her a few minutes ago. He'd been so careful not to look at her face, but now it was too late.

Her auburn hair formed a cloud around her face, the waves never quite tamed. Her eyes were a punch in the gut, the exact shade of green of moss growing on a river rock, deep and vibrant. Their expression stopped his breath every time.

She had old eyes, the eyes of someone who'd lived several lifetimes. Always tinged with a hint of sadness, like she'd seen and heard too much.

"I'm sorry," he repeated. Words had never been his strong suit, and he'd never wished more that he could say things better.

"Not your fault. It's horrible weather." Her tone had returned to reasonable and calm. She'd gotten herself under control, and he wished he could say the same for his insides.

"I'm assuming we're stuck?" She waved her hand in the direction of the driver's side window, indicating the snowdrift swallowing the back left half of her car and the left side of the truck.

19

He cleared his throat. "I think so. I mean, we can try again if you want …"

"I don't know if I can do that again."

"Let me take a look at the other side at least."

He walked around the back end of the car, and yeah, it would take a truck with more horsepower than his pickup to get them out. Or a few hours of shoveling.

He went back to her passenger window. "I don't think we're getting out of this without another tow."

"Great. A tow truck for the tow truck." She shook her head, reached across the seat for her bag, and rolled up her window, shutting him out for a moment.

Through the glass, he watched her crawl over the gearshift and pop open the passenger door.

"At least the airbag didn't deploy."

She was trying to sound upbeat, look for the positive in all this, which only made it worse. He'd come here to do one nice thing for her, and made a mess of everything again. She'd have been better off waiting for the professional tow truck to come.

"Yeah. Lucky thing. Look, I'm sorry I tried to tow you. I should've—"

She cut him off with a wave of her hand. "It's done now. We'll have to wait inside for the tow truck."

"Inside," he repeated. He'd imagined himself waiting in the pickup for the next few hours.

"Yes. There's heat in there. Unlike out here."

"I can stay out here," he said quickly. "You go on in."

She squinted at him through the swirling snow. She had to be freezing by now in her thin coat and those pointy-heeled boots she favored.

"Stay out here. In your truck. When it's well below freezing."

"If that's what you wanted—"

"I'm pissed off at you, but I don't want you to die of hypothermia."

"I wouldn't—" He cleared his throat. "Okay. I'll get a couple of things."

It was easier to agree than argue with her. What couple of things he needed to get was also a mystery, but he needed a break from her gaze, and the sudden realization that they were about to be alone together for the first time in months.

She followed on his heels as he went to the truck's passenger door, the snow coming halfway to her knees now. He kept his eyes down. But he shouldn't have looked at her boots a minute ago. They were basically high heels in boot form, and they called to mind the red, fuck-me pumps she'd been wearing the day they'd met. He'd never met a woman who wore shoes like that in real life.

Even with the shoes, she didn't clear his chin. Not even close, and he was only a little taller than average at six foot one. Vanessa was all of five feet and one half inches tall, and she'd never let him forget the extra half inch.

This was very bad. He'd just had to come here tonight, and this was the result. But if he hadn't come here tonight, she'd be alone in this mess. Even worse.

He yanked the truck's door open, climbed inside, and killed the ignition. From the backseat, he retrieved his first aid kit, emergency blanket, and water bottle. Vanessa waited by the door, her eyebrow raised.

"We have food and water inside, you know. You're not going camping."

"I know." He needed something to do with his hands, some kind of purpose to direct his actions.

But it was freezing out here, the snow not letting up, and she needed to get inside. He slid out of the seat and onto the snow-packed pavement next to her, but not before she glanced up into the truck cab and saw the flowers on the front seat.

She froze, her eyes widening. Yeah, they were her favorite flower, and he'd known that when he picked them out, and she knew he knew that. A second later, her expression shuttered, and she looked over her shoulder toward the clinic.

"Hurry up. I'm freezing."

Without waiting for his reply, she turned and marched across the lot toward the porch. On the first step, her heel slipped and she almost went down, but she grabbed the railing and righted herself at the last minute.

"Okay?" He hadn't made it close enough to catch her in time.

"I'm fine," she huffed. "It's really slippery."

"Your shoes don't help."

"My shoes are seasonally appropriate."

He snorted and followed her up the steps.

She rounded on him, key in the door. "What?"

"Nothing."

"You're laughing at my shoes."

He sobered. "I'm not laughing at them." They were one of a thousand things that made Vanessa the hottest woman he'd ever seen.

"They're just not … They're not …" He gave up and shook his head. Kept his mouth shut, which worked best for him most times.

She turned her back on him and yanked on the door with her whole miniscule weight. The thing creaked open, half-blocked by ice from the earlier freezing rain.

"I can help."

"No, I've got it." One more pull and she had it open.

Then they were inside the foyer, and the sudden silence and warmth enveloped them. The wind must have been howling harder than he'd realized, because now his own breath seemed too loud in his ears.

This place smelled familiar, the homey scent of Vanessa's favorite too-expensive candles mingling with leftover wood smoke from the antique fireplace. They'd met here, when she'd called his shop, looking for someone to fix the clinic's dishwasher. They'd talked here in her office after their first meeting, and then she'd asked him out, which had blown his mind.

Because how could a woman like her have an interest in an appliance repairman with a dad bod and patches on his canvas work pants? But she had been interested, for whatever reason, and she'd asked him out.

The next three months had been a dream. Until it had all come crashing down, thanks to him. Well, thanks to Silvia giving him the scare of a lifetime.

They stood facing one another, him frozen in the memories, and her looking at him with her penetrating stare. The one that let her see through people, as part of her job. Professional seer-through-er.

"Well. Might as well get warmed up. My socks are wet."

She turned her back on him and slid her coat down her shoulders, and he did not offer to help. After hanging it on a coat hook, she sat on the bench by the door and unzipped her black heeled boots, slid the first one off her foot, and went to work peeling down the tall, sheer socks she wore underneath.

He jerked his gaze away from her and shoved his hands in his pockets. This was worse than awkward. Nowhere to look but at her. No place to escape the conversation they were about to have.

And they were about to have a conversation. He could feel it brewing under the surface. With Vanessa, it was always talking about feelings. Working on good communication. She was an expert in that, and in the short time they'd dated, she'd pried more words out of him than anyone else ever had. So no, she would not let this opportunity go.

She surprised him by standing and walking past him without a word, down the hall toward the kitchen located on the back side of the old house.

"You want tea?" she asked, tossing the words over her shoulder.

He toed off his work boots, hung up his coat, and followed her, silent.

Don't look at her too much, and then maybe you can tell her the truth.

He'd never wished more he was the man she needed, the one who was good at communicating. Maybe then he could tell her why he'd stopped texting her, how much Silvia had needed him, but how that hadn't made it any easier.

Maybe Vanessa could even forgive him. The thought curled in his gut, a wisp of longing. He'd missed her. Hadn't known how much until he'd laid eyes on her, and his heart lurched into motion again after months of feeling dead.

At the doorway of the kitchen, he stood in silence and watched her fill the electric kettle, plug it in, and extract mugs from the cabinet. She was so short without her heels, she had to stand on tiptoe to reach the average-height shelving. He did not offer to help, because she'd only say no.

The kettle rumbled as it heated, and she turned, leaned back, and braced her hands on the counter behind her.

"So, who were the flowers for?" she asked, fixing her gaze on him.

Her tone was mild, but he froze in place, throat tightening. This was the point in every conversation where he said the wrong thing, put his foot in his mouth, and made the situation worse. One of many reasons why he didn't talk much.

He made himself meet her eyes as his brain scrambled for an answer.

"I ... They're yours. If you want them. But they're dead now."

Chapter 3

Vanessa's brain ticked through the possible meanings of Noah's statement. Maybe he'd bought the flowers for someone else, but now that he was stuck here, he was offering them to her.

Roses were her favorite flower, but they were also pretty standard Valentine's Day gifts. Except these roses had been fuchsia. Not as common as red, and also her preferred color. So he'd bought her exact favorite flower for someone else.

Or, he'd bought them for her, but he'd forgotten about them after tossing them in his truck, and then they'd died. Maybe he didn't want to give her dead flowers. Or maybe he did. Getting direct information out of this man was like shouting through a brick wall.

Anyway, the roses were frozen, and not worth rescuing or talking about. Especially if he couldn't even walk in here and hand them to her. If they'd even been intended for her in the first place.

"I don't want them," she said. She busied herself pouring hot water over the tea bags to brew their tea.

His long inhale filled the space, but he didn't reply.

In the quiet warmth of the kitchen, he seemed to take up more space. His broad frame filled the doorway, all wide shoulders, thick thighs, and firm, rounded belly.

He took up a lot of physical space, but energy-wise, he'd always been calming to her. His solid warmth had a dampening effect on the edges of her anxiety. He'd always been easy to be around, those flannel shirts soft against her face when he pulled her into a hug.

She drew herself up straight, bracing against those unwanted feelings. She turned and handed him his mug, fixing a neutral expression on her face.

"I *am* curious to know what you were doing here in the first place, this late on a weeknight," she said.

He held the mug without drinking and looked at her for a long minute. It took him a while to come up with words, but she'd wait while he went through his process.

"I came by because ... I knew tonight was important to you."

She set down her cup. He was full of unexpected, confusing statements tonight. "Can you explain that any more?"

"It's Valentine's Day tomorrow. Your favorite day."

"It is my favorite day." Or it used to be. Before love had kicked her in the pants a few too many times.

She used to go all-out, decorating her home and office as thoroughly as some people decorated for Christmas. She'd make Valentine's Day cookies, and wear a themed outfit, and always, always, plan her biggest date night of the year.

But she hadn't done any of those things this year. Last year at this time, she'd still been with Noah.

When she didn't offer anything else, he went on. "And so I

thought … I just thought I'd check in on you."

"So you did buy those flowers for me."

His brows lowered. "That's what I said."

"No you didn't. You said I could have them if I wanted them. That's different."

"I didn't mean …" He trailed off. Looked down into his mug, as if it held answers for him.

"Do you want to sit down?" She tilted her head toward the kitchen table, and he gave a miserable-looking nod. She almost felt sorry for him, until she reminded herself what he'd done. The ghosting, and the six-word text.

With the table between them, she felt better. Stronger. Ready to face this conversation happening ten months too late.

"So you came by to do what? Check in on me? You were going to drop the flowers and run?"

His expression shifted, confirming her suspicions.

"You were. That's what you were going to do. Drive-by flowers. You didn't want to see me or talk to me."

"It's not that I didn't want to. I didn't know what I'd say. I know I can't fix things, so I figured there was no point in trying to talk about it."

She sat back in her chair. This was more information than she'd had the last ten months, and her therapist brain latched onto every hidden meaning.

"Do you want to fix things?" she asked.

"Stop." He set the mug down a little too hard, startling her.

"Stop what?"

"Stop rearranging what I said. I said I know I can't fix it. There isn't any chance of making it better."

"But you're still thinking about it." Maybe he'd thought about it as much as she had.

A pained expression crossed his features, and an answering pang hit her in the solar plexus. This didn't look like a man who'd been happy to dump her when someone else came along.

"I can't do this." He stood abruptly, pushing his chair back. "Nothing about my situation has changed."

He strode out of the kitchen, and she jumped up and followed on his heels, taking two steps for every one of his.

"Where are you going?"

"Back to the truck. I'll wait in the cab."

"Noah, wait. Please stop. Will you listen to me for a minute?"

He froze with his hand on the knob.

"I didn't mean to push you. But what you just said. About your situation not changing. You never told me your situation in the first place. I'm still in the dark, and I'd like to know what happened. That's not asking a lot."

"I know." His chin dropped, and he refused to meet her eyes.

"When you broke up with me, all you said was 'it would be for the best.' So I assumed that meant you'd met someone else."

"What? No." His tone sharpened, and he spun to face her. "I wouldn't … That's not …" He shook his head, clearly reaching for words. *"That's* what you thought?"

"Well, yeah. Of course." She shrugged. "Usually, when people ghost you, and things had been going pretty well up until that point, it means they met someone else."

Noah's eyes slammed shut and his chest rose with a couple of deep inhales. When he opened them, the look he directed at her was searing. His big brown eyes, normally soft and deep, held a strange intensity, and she couldn't look away.

"That wasn't the reason why," he said.

"Okay." Her voice came out breathless. "Then why?"

"I can't explain it to you."

"I promise you, I've heard everything. Secret double identity?" she asked, trying to lighten the mood and failing.

"No."

"You have a foot fetish. Which I kind of already knew, for the record."

A dull red crept up into his face. "It's not that."

That left another possibility, the one most likely to be true.

"Then you chickened out. You didn't want to get so close, so fast. Or maybe I came on too strong."

She said the words as matter-of-factly as possible, as if they wouldn't hurt the worst of all, if they turned out to be true. She had a hard time opening up, but when she did, she could be … a lot of personality to handle.

"It wasn't that either," he said, his tone low.

"But you're not going to tell me what was going on. What is apparently still going on, and preventing us from having an honest conversation."

"You know I'm not good at this." He made a gesture in the air between them, indicating the having of conversations.

"I know." She huffed out a sigh. "And it looks like you don't want to try to change that."

His silence gave her the answer she needed.

"Okay. I guess, after ten months, you don't owe me an explanation. We aren't involved with each other anymore. It's close to midnight, and I'm tired. I'll get you a blanket and you can pick a couch. You don't even have to see me again tonight. But don't sleep in your car, okay? I don't want your death on my conscience."

"Okay."

One word wrapped up this strange conversation, in which she'd still learned nothing at all. Except he hadn't cheated on her, and he still liked her feet.

"Good." She gave a brief nod and went upstairs to the closet where they kept extra throw pillows and blankets, leaving him still standing by the front door, frozen in place.

The Well Space had three floors, three sitting rooms, and fourteen treatment rooms. There was enough space that she could avoid him for a few hours, probably until morning if she was realistic on the tow truck timeline. Then she'd get her car unstuck and never see him again. The smartest and best option for both of them.

You couldn't have a conversation with another person determined to put up a wall between you. Just like you couldn't have a relationship with one person who wouldn't participate.

Relationships ended for all kinds of reasons. As soon as she spotted a red flag, she'd found it best to get out, before everything got worse. She'd seen firsthand the results of staying in a bad relationship, and no thank you to that.

For the past ten months, she hadn't dated at all—her longest dry spell in … ever. Maybe it was time to give up on the dream of romantic love for herself.

But Noah had seemed horrified at her assumption he'd been cheating. That reaction had been genuine, and anyway, he was a terrible liar. He was also a terrible talker, period.

Still, what she'd thought she understood about their breakup had crumbled under examination, leaving her wondering what their foundation had been. Had she known anything real about him at all?

She pulled a large throw blanket from the closet and headed downstairs, where she found him still standing by the front door, looking uncomfortable. He'd rather sleep in his truck in sub-freezing weather than talk to her.

"The downstairs couch is the biggest," she told him, and motioned for him to follow her. The less talking, the better.

She heard his footsteps behind her in the hallway as she led him to the downstairs sitting room. A large leather couch she'd found at an estate sale dominated the space, next to the fireplace, where a few embers glowed.

"You can add more wood to the fireplace if you want," she said.

"No, thank you. I'll be fine."

"Okay." She tossed the blanket on the couch. "I'll be in my office, then. Second floor, if you need anything."

"I remember where it is."

He sat on the couch and looked up at her through his lashes. God, she'd forgotten how long his eyelashes were. Like extensions, or what you'd find on a doll. He had doe eyes, soft and sweet. Her fingers remembered the softness of his dark beard, too, and she smoothed them down the sides of her skirt.

He held her gaze a beat longer before speaking, like he wanted to make sure she was paying attention.

"I never would have cheated on you," he said, his voice full of gravel.

"Okay." Her breath suspended in her chest as the words hung in the air between them. Maybe she'd misunderstood. There was something about the situation she hadn't seen—

"But there was … someone. Someone who I had to … They needed a lot of my time." He broke eye contact and shifted on the couch, looking miserable.

"I see," she snapped. She didn't, in fact, see what he meant at all. But the underlying meaning was clear. Someone else had been more important, important enough for him to end his relationship.

32

Chapter 3

"I didn't mean—"

"I'm not sure I want to hear any more right now. You're not going to tell me all the details anyway, right?"

His shoulders slumped. "I guess not."

"Then I'm heading upstairs."

Any longer in this quiet room with him looking at her like that, she was bound to do something stupid like believe he had good intentions, or forgive him.

"Okay. Thanks for the blanket."

She gave him a quick nod and escaped upstairs to her office. Everything was where she'd left it a couple of hours earlier, and she wouldn't be falling asleep anytime soon. Might as well take some more notes from her recordings.

But instead of sitting at her desk, she paced the room, her bare feet like ice on the cold wood floor. Now it was the night before Valentine's Day, and not only was she stuck at work, her ex-boyfriend was asleep downstairs.

Being a hopeless romantic only got you so far. At a certain point, reality came crashing in, along with the understanding that most men were walking red flags. If it wasn't one thing, it was another. If she had any standards at all, she'd forget the stricken expression on Noah's face a few minutes ago.

Maybe he'd been about to say something different, and it had come out wrong. But whatever he'd been about to say, it couldn't explain his behavior. People made time for the people they loved. If he'd cared enough about her, whatever else had been going on in his life wouldn't have stopped him from being with her.

And since she hadn't been his priority then, she wouldn't be now. She'd have to ignore his soft eyes and cozy-looking flannel shirt, and she would not go downstairs to check on him, to see if he looked as peaceful asleep as she remembered.

In the morning, she'd say goodbye to him as quickly as possible. She'd move on with her personal and professional life, and help other people, so that they never, ever had to feel like this. Because this feeling was the worst.

"Good," she said aloud in the quiet office.

She reached for the reading lamp on her desk, twisted the old-fashioned brass switch at the base of it, and it flashed on, illuminating the space. Two seconds later, the power cut out, and the entire building went dark and silent.

Chapter 4

The stairs squeaked under his feet as Noah made his way upstairs, holding onto the railing in the pitch black. He'd heard Vanessa pacing around above his head, then when the power went out, silence.

She wasn't afraid of the dark. She didn't need him to come upstairs and make sure she was okay. But that didn't change the fact that as soon as the lights had gone out, he'd jumped off the couch to go to her. Maybe he was the one who needed reassurance.

But also, the house was old, poorly insulated, and the space was about to get a lot colder. He'd make sure she had enough blankets. At any rate, the upstairs of the house was bound to be warmer than downstairs, as the heat rose from the dying coals in the fireplace.

"Vanessa?"

It made no sense that he'd whispered the word, but the dark amplified every sound, and a normal-volume statement would have sounded like a shout in the silence blanketing the house.

"I'm here. Third door on the left."

"I remember." As if he could have forgotten.

A minute later, he stuck his head in the door of her office. She sat on the couch, her face illuminated by the glow of her phone.

"I just reported the outage to the power company," she said. "Looks like the whole downtown area is out."

"Figured. The wind is pretty bad. Must have knocked a branch onto a power line."

"Yeah." She sighed and clicked the phone off. "I signed up for updates, but they don't even have an estimated time it's coming back on."

"I imagine they're pretty busy tonight."

"Yep."

She didn't offer any further comment.

"So …" He stopped, cleared his throat. "You're doing okay up here?"

"Uh-huh. Totally fine. You can go back downstairs if you want."

"What if I don't want to?"

Her head whipped around. In the pale light coming in the window—the moon reflecting off the snow—he caught her dumbfounded expression.

"You want to stay up here?"

"If you don't mind. I could sit with you. We could share the blanket." He held up the comforter he'd dragged up the stairs with him.

"I am not cuddling with you," she said tightly.

"I didn't mean that," he hurried on. "I just meant we could sit together. It's big enough to cover us both, and it's about to get cold."

36

Her indrawn breath carried across the space. "Okay. Fine."

He sat on the opposite end of the couch from her. It was a small piece of furniture, more of a loveseat, the fabric plush under his fingers. He pulled the blanket over himself, lifted the edge, and offered it to her.

She took the corner of the blanket he offered and pulled it up to her chin, curling her legs under her on the couch.

"Thanks. My feet have been freezing since I took off my socks."

He'd forgotten she didn't have socks. But now the memory of her pale foot with its bright red nail polish flashed in front of his eyes, and he pushed the image away, because now was not the time to remember those details.

"You can put your feet on me if you want." That came out wrong, too. Like almost everything he said around her.

"Noah. I'm not putting my foot on your leg right now."

"It's cold. And I'm wearing jeans. It's not like I'm going to feel anything."

"You know what? You deserve icy feet on your leg."

She extended both feet across the loveseat and shoved them under his thigh, and he'd been wrong. Her feet were so cold, he could in fact feel them through the denim.

"Ohhh, that is nice." Her head went back on the couch cushion behind her, and she wiggled her toes.

A shock of sensation went up his spine from the place they touched. She had to be doing that to torture him, and not to warm up her feet. But he couldn't take back his offer now.

He hadn't forgotten the strength of their physical connection, but it had been so long. In this one thing, they were perfectly matched. Words were hard, but touch was a language they did well.

He sucked in a breath, then another, bracing against the wave of sheer want. Images flashed in front of his mind, of him pulling her into his lap, kissing her here in the dark, where it wouldn't matter they weren't together anymore, because they were here right now. His fist clenched on the thigh of his jeans.

He couldn't see her clearly in the dim light, the moon shining in the window. Maybe that was why words tumbled out of him now. Because of the dark, and her touching him again for the first time in months.

"I want to tell you why I broke it off with you. The whole story," he added.

Her head lifted off the cushion, regarding him in silence. She didn't say anything, letting him pick his way through the words.

"My parents broke up last year. It was really sudden. My mom ... She showed up on my doorstep one night with a suitcase. She's always been headstrong. She walked out on my dad and took the fucking city bus to my apartment, rather than call me. Said she didn't need a ride, and she'd only stay for one night."

He shook his head at the memory, breathing through some of the tension curling in his gut. That night had destroyed a lot of things he counted on. He tried to focus on the important part, the part Vanessa needed to know to understand why he'd broken up with her.

"I talked her into staying with me for a while, until she figured out what she wants to do next. She's been ... She's not in good health. And I owed it to her to help her out."

Vanessa was silent for a moment before speaking. "I'm sorry to hear about your parents. But are you saying you ghosted me because of a family emergency? Why didn't you just tell me? Instead of never texting me again."

His jaw ticked. "It's hard to explain."

"Please try."

"I had about a week where my house was pure chaos. Dad calling every hour. Mom swearing up and down she wouldn't talk to him. It was …" He slammed his eyes shut. "It was a lot to deal with. And the more time passed, the worse I felt not texting you. But I didn't want you to see all that. I hoped it would get resolved in a few days."

"I understand if it was family business, and you didn't want to tell me all the details. But you could have told me *something*."

He shook his head. "I know that now. But I was too …"

Devastated. He'd been devastated and scared out of his mind, and he hadn't wanted to show himself to Vanessa in that state. She deserved to have him in better shape. He hadn't wanted that ugliness to touch the perfection of what they'd shared so far.

"I didn't want to involve you," he finished lamely.

He heard her slow indrawn breath. "You didn't think you could count on me to be there for you?"

"It's not that. I didn't want you to see me like that." Closer to the truth.

"When I texted you. After two weeks of silence," she added. "I said, 'It seems like you want to take a break.' And you said, 'That would be for the best.'"

He winced at the repetition of his own stupid sentence.

"I'm sorry. I thought maybe it was."

He'd been swamped with guilt for not returning her messages, and the creeping fear he wasn't good enough to keep her, that he didn't deserve her. His life had gotten too complicated and too out of hand.

Now, in this quiet room, the words seemed like not nearly enough.

"I see," she said. But her tone said she didn't see.

"I'm not making excuses. I don't think I handled any of it very well." Or at all. "But she's still living with me now, and things haven't gotten better with my parents. So maybe you wouldn't have wanted to be with me through all that."

"You didn't ask me if I wanted to. You made this into a choice between me and your family, all in your own head." Vanessa shook her head in disbelief.

"I didn't mean to."

"Whatever you meant, that is what you did." She punctuated her sentence with a jab of her foot against his leg. "Your family and your girlfriend did not have to be in competition with one another."

She sucked in a sharp breath. "Red flags. Every time. I don't know how I manage to do this to myself over and over."

"It wasn't your fault."

She had been the one who'd suggested they break up, technically. But he'd agreed to it far too quickly. And he'd been the one doing the ghosting in the first place. This was more on him than her.

Maybe things would have been fine, if he'd explained his situation to her. She might even have thought of a better solution than the one he'd come up with so far, which was to beg Silvia to take Dad's calls or talk to a therapist. With no success.

He shut his eyes, reaching for calm, trying with his full strength not to reach out and put a hand on her leg. This was what he got for trying to communicate.

Chapter 4

Vanessa stayed silent, seeming lost in thought. After a moment, she turned her head on the couch cushion to look at him in the dim light.

"The stupid thing is, I don't even blame you. Family is important. But you could have at least *told* me."

"I'm sorry."

"You hurt me." Her voice changed, becoming smaller and softer.

His heart accelerated, rushing in his ears, because she was the last person he'd ever wanted to hurt and he'd done it anyway. His parents' disaster of a separation had reached out and hurt her anyway, the very thing he'd tried to avoid.

He couldn't talk himself out of a paper bag, and this was one more result of it.

"I'm sorry," he repeated.

"And what about what you wanted? Did you even want to break up with me, or did you just let it happen?"

"I ..." He swallowed, uncertain of what to say next and certain whatever he said, it would be wrong. If he told her he'd never wanted to lose her, that it had nearly killed him, how much worse would she hate him for ruining everything?

"Can't say it, huh," she said, her tone dull.

He shook his head.

"All right." She flopped her head back again. "Well, I'm glad you told me why, at least. Thanks for being honest."

He swallowed again, trying to ease the tightness in his throat. Talking got you nowhere. She was no closer to understanding the inside of him than she had been before this conversation. She'd only gotten the external details of his circumstances.

"You were right earlier," he said, looking down at his hands. "When you guessed I was planning to drop off the flowers and

41

leave."

"I know."

"I didn't want to talk to you tonight. But I'm glad you know now. I mean, I'm not glad I hurt you."

"Noah. Can we stop talking now?"

"Yeah." He'd done it again, the words coming out twisted and wrong.

She was silent for several minutes, so quiet he thought she'd fallen asleep. Then her phone screen lit up as she checked the time.

"1:00 a.m. Happy Valentine's Day to us." She dropped the phone back into the blanket.

"Happy Valentine's."

"Remember last year?" she asked softly.

"Don't," he nearly groaned.

"We had a nice time, didn't we? At least for a while." She sounded wistful and a little sad, and he wanted to pull her over to him, wrap her in his arms, and feel her against him one more time.

"Yeah. We did."

"I'm going to try to sleep for a bit. With any luck, the power will come back in a couple hours. The tow truck company texted they'd be even later getting here."

"Okay."

She turned her torso away from him, leaving her feet shoved under his thigh, and curled up in a ball with her head on the armrest. She looked even tinier like that, small enough he could easily pick her up, but she'd never allowed that, back when they'd been together. She'd always demanded he respect the autonomy of all ninety-eight pounds of her body, and he'd always given that respect.

She fell silent, leaving him awake with memories of this night last year. She'd worn a short, tight velvet dress, somewhere between red and pink. Screamingly bright with matching heels and her hair forming a halo around her head. They'd gone out to dinner at a restaurant she'd researched and reserved a month ahead of time.

Afterward, she'd pulled him into the narrow alley behind the restaurant and kissed him until his teeth ached. He'd wrapped her inside his work coat and felt her up, even though people walked right past the entrance to the hidden alcove.

When he'd told her they'd better stop, she'd laughed and unzipped his fly, bringing him off in a dozen magnificent strokes, and if he hadn't admitted to himself he loved her before that night, he did at that moment.

He loved her fearlessness and brightness, her intelligence and compassion. Her smoking hot skills in bed were the icing on the cake.

But life had given him things that seemed nice, and then life took those things away. He'd always known he had to be ready to give up the people and things he loved, because nothing was safe from change. Not his parents, and not his relationships.

It hadn't been easy to let her go. He wanted to shake her awake and tell her. He'd tell her it was the last thing he'd wanted. He hadn't been thinking clearly, had been trying to manage the crisis and do his duty as a son, and keep all of it far, far away from Vanessa. The only way he could be worthy of her was to be that man, the one who took care of his obligations and held everything together.

But none of those words would ever come out of his mouth in the right order.

He sighed and pulled the blanket up to his shoulders. The

dark room grew colder, and Vanessa's soft breathing evened out into sleep. She'd never had problems sleeping around him, even though he probably shook the bed and bounced her frame around every time he moved. They'd fit together perfectly, in fact, two nesting dolls.

He shut his eyes and let himself drift, focusing his attention on the connection between her foot and his leg.

He woke up some time later, not to the power coming back on or the light of morning, but to jerky movements from Vanessa's side of the couch. His eyes snapped open in the dark, and he found her curled in an even tighter ball than before, if that was possible. She'd covered her head with both arms, and the movements he'd felt were her flinching, over and over, as if being struck.

"Vanessa." He put a hand on her arm.

She'd never had a nightmare around him before. When the hand on her arm didn't wake her, he rested his palm on her back, gently, so as not to startle her.

She came awake on a gasp, uncurling fast as he hurried to draw his hand away. Her sharp inhales cut through the silence.

"You were having a bad dream," he told her.

"Yeah. Sorry. Did I wake you up?"

"It's fine. Not like I was sleeping that deep."

"No. I wasn't either."

"What were you dreaming about?"

"Just an old dream. It comes back sometimes. I'm okay." Without looking at him, she curled up and turned away from him again, shutting him out.

He closed his eyes again. He wouldn't go back to sleep, and neither would she. In an hour or two, the sun would be up, and this whole nightmare of an evening would be over.

Chapter 4

He'd accomplished exactly nothing by coming here, other than crashing his truck, humiliating himself, and confirming that his relationship, the one he'd ended with his own negligence, was indeed dead.

He startled a minute later when he felt her hand on his arm. She'd reached behind her, placed her palm on his bicep, and curled her small fingers into his sleeve. She left it there as she drifted back to sleep.

Chapter 5

Vanessa woke to sunlight streaming in the window and a feeling of being toasty warm. Too warm, considering she was in an unheated room, a fact she knew because her nose was cold.

She cracked open her eyes to find that in her sleep, she'd turned to Noah and cuddled him like a giant teddy bear. She opened her eyes slowly, being careful not to move as she inhaled his smell of laundry detergent and engine grease. He must have gotten oil on his clothing while hooking her car to his truck.

Last night came back to her in a rush, and she let the feelings wash through her—sadness, a wish things had turned out different. But not as much anger. Some of that had drained out of her.

Noah's beard looked so soft, his bottom lip fuller than the top one. He frowned in his sleep, like he was concentrating hard on something in his dream, and it had the effect of making him look younger. It wouldn't take much to close the gap between their faces.

Kissing someone in their sleep, without their permission, wasn't a great way to establish trust in a relationship. And they didn't have a relationship anymore. He was probably frowning because he couldn't wait to get out of here and get away from her.

Still, she drew in a full breath for what felt like the first time in months, her body warm and calm. He'd always had that effect on her, her own personal anti-anxiety medication.

His eyes opened and he looked at her, sleepy and disoriented. For a moment, his expression was open and fond, the way he used to look at her when they'd just woken up, like seeing her first thing in the morning was the best thing to ever happen to him.

His expression propelled her forward, and she touched her lips to his. His inhale cut the silence, his eyes sharp on her face, and she pulled back fast.

"I'm sorry. I'm not sure what I was thinking," she said.

His eyes searched hers, as if he could read what was going on inside her. And good luck to him figuring it out, because she had no idea why she'd done that.

Then he surged up and kissed her, for real this time, and God, she'd missed this. His mouth hot and soft against hers, moving with insistent pressure until she let him inside. As soon as she parted her lips, he was there, stroking into her mouth and sending her spiraling into a well of heat.

They shouldn't do this, but shouldn't was a very weak word in the face of ten months of pent-up longing. She'd missed him. She hadn't let herself miss him, but now that his mouth was on her, the missing poured out of her in a giant rush. She looped her arms around him and pulled him closer.

He seemed to feel the same way, starved and insistent. He pulled her up until she sprawled on his wide chest. She put her fingers into the soft, thick fur of his beard and let herself melt further into pulsing sweetness.

Neither of them would stop this. The dim thought flashed in the back of her mind, a shorted-out bulb. They'd keep going until he took her right here on the couch, in her office, where she sat with her clients and talked about their relationships in a professional capacity.

The warning bells chimed louder and she ripped her mouth from his, panting as if she'd run a mile. Noah looked wrecked, his hair standing up, mouth open and red. She wanted to dive back into the kiss and take it where it had been headed a minute ago.

But someone had to stop this insanely bad idea. And in the past, that someone had never been her. She'd jumped into bed with men too quickly, and it had never ended well for her yet.

He was her ex. He'd broken up with her for questionable reasons, and he'd been stuck here with her last night against his will. This was not a healthy way to repair a relationship.

And he didn't want to repair it anyway. He'd said nothing of the kind last night. Not that she'd trust him farther than she could throw a stick, even if he had.

She stood in a rush, taking a big step back from the couch, then winced at the shock of the temperature change.

"God damn, the floor is cold."

He'd been staring at her, dazed, but her words jolted him into action.

"Here." He leaned over, peeled off his socks, and handed them to her. "They're clean. Probably six sizes too big, though."

"You don't have to give me your socks."

"Will you take them?" He was still breathless from the kiss, flustered. "Let me just … Let me do one thing for you."

"Okay." She took the thick wool socks from him and slid them on. They were still warm from his body heat. "Thank you."

"So. Uh." He scrubbed a hand over his hair. "About what just happened."

"I shouldn't have kissed you. It was an impulse, and I'm sorry if I gave you the wrong impression."

"The wrong impression," he said cautiously.

"We're not getting back together. That's not why you came here. And we didn't settle anything last night."

"We didn't." He seemed capable only of echoing her.

She gave a sharp nod. "All right, then. We agree. I'm going to call the tow place and check where I am in line. I also need to check the sinks downstairs. We get frozen pipes sometimes in the winter, and there's been no heat for hours."

"I'll check the pipes for you." He jumped up from the couch. "I can shovel the walkway, too. Maybe shovel around the truck so there's a path when the tow truck gets here."

"Good idea."

He gave her a wide berth as they headed to her office door, but he paused at the door frame.

"What's with all the equipment on your desk?"

"Oh. I'm starting a podcast. About relationships. That's all my recording stuff."

He rubbed the back of his neck. "You'll be good at that."

"Glad you think so." She gave a nervous laugh, and they headed to the staircase like awkward coworkers, rather than two people who'd been making out.

She stopped halfway down the stairs as the view out the

49

front windows emerged.

"Look at that."

The world had been transformed into a snowy wonderland. A thick layer of white blanketed the trees and the front porch, the whole yard bright and silent, a winter postcard.

She felt him come up behind her and resisted the urge to lean back into him.

"It's so pretty," she said. "I bet we got close to two feet of snow last night."

"Yeah. It's pretty when you're not driving in it. Even better when you have heat."

She shivered. "Yeah, I'm going to put my coat on."

"I can make a fire if you want?"

"That would be smart. It could be another few hours until they get here."

He went to do his self-assigned jobs, and Vanessa pulled on her coat and took her phone to the kitchen to make the calls. She sent an email to The Well Space staff, telling everyone to stay home today, in case they hadn't already figured it out. Therapy appointments would be changed to video calls or rescheduled.

Then she called the towing company, and as it turned out, there was only a ninety-minute wait for a tow truck. Ninety minutes until it was time to say goodbye to Noah.

She needed caffeine, and had no way to boil water. She rummaged around in the cabinets until she found a glass jar of instant coffee. Noah poked his head in the kitchen door as she was considering dissolving the bitter powder in hot tap water.

"Pipes are good," he said.

"Good to hear. The tow truck will be here in a little over an hour."

"Fire's going, too, if you want to sit there while you wait."

"I do. I'm trying to decide if I'm desperate enough to drink lukewarm instant coffee."

He lifted a shoulder. "Better than nothing."

"You're right." She gave a decisive nod, heaped the powder into two mugs, and added tap water. She handed a mug to him.

"You've got to try it, too."

"Okay."

He took the mug from her, and they sat on the couch by the fireplace in the front foyer, where she'd left him alone last night. This night had stretched on forever, and it couldn't be over soon enough. She took a sip of the bitter coffee, winced, and set the mug on the end table.

He cleared his throat. "So you're doing a podcast about relationships."

"I'm just getting it started. Haven't even taped the first episode. But yeah, I hope to help more people than the clients I see in person. It'll be more general relationship advice, not really counseling."

"That's a good idea." His brows went down. "I should tell my mom to listen to it. She might learn a few things."

"What would you want her to learn?" She couldn't help pressing for more information. Carefully, so he didn't clam up.

"To work things out with my Dad," he said, as if that was the obvious solution.

"People change over time. It's not always possible to stay together, and that can be part of the process, too."

"Of course I know that. I just think they belong together."

He seemed pretty set on his parents getting back together.

But things didn't always work out that way.

Noah surprised her by continuing to talk.

"My mom's stubborn. She doesn't like to ask for help. I'm trying to give her space to figure herself out, but nothing's changing."

She tilted her head to the side, regarding him. "I don't know your mom. In fact, you never told me much about your parents at all. But I do know you need to respect her process."

"Her process is ridiculous."

"All of us are ridiculous sometimes, especially in our relationships. None of us knows what's best in the moment. Sometimes until it's too late."

His gaze burned into her, suddenly more intense. "I guess we are kind of ridiculous."

"So let her figure it out."

"Not like she gives me a choice." He lifted his chin toward the front window. "There's the truck. They're early. I'll go help him out. Then you can get out of here."

She watched him put his bare feet into his work boots, slide on his coat, and head outside into the snow for the second time this morning.

He hadn't said another word about the kiss. No mention of how good it had been, or if it had reminded him of how things had been between them. If it had made him rethink what he'd done ten months ago.

Inside his head, all of his own actions made sense. The reasons he'd ghosted her. The reasons he'd shown up here last night with flowers, but no plans of talking to her. The reasons he'd kissed her brains out on a hair trigger.

He was the one who needed therapy. He needed someone to point out to him that his actions were contradictory and made no sense.

She carried both mugs to the kitchen and rinsed them in the sink. At the front door, she removed Noah's socks, folded them into a neat ball, and put on her own narrow boots barefoot. Then she waited by the front door, watching the progress of the tow truck as it extracted first Noah's pickup, then her SUV, from the corner of the parking lot.

Twenty minutes later, the tow truck sped off, leaving Noah sitting in the cab of his truck. Was he going to drive off? His truck was blocking her car, so he'd have to leave before she did. It would be typical of him to leave her without another word at this point.

But he didn't leave. He sat there in the truck cab, staring at the bench seat next to him, his breath making plumes in the freezing air. Then he got out of the truck and slammed the door. In his hand he held a single pink rose from the bouquet he'd brought last night.

Her heart cinched at the sight of him coming up the porch steps, bright flower in hand, looking like a lumberjack getting ready to ask out a prom date. She pulled the door open as he got closer.

"This one didn't die." He frowned in confusion at the flower in his hand. "I'm not sure why. Maybe because it's right around freezing tcmp out here. But the whole rest of the bouquet died, and right in the middle was this one flower. Still alive."

He held it out to her silently, and she took it, handing him his balled-up socks in exchange.

"I think this means I was supposed to give you those flowers," he said. "So I'm doing what I should have done from the start last night."

He cleared his throat. "Vanessa, I'm sorry for what I did. I

53

know I hurt you, and I know this doesn't make it okay. But I did get those flowers for you. Because I couldn't stop thinking about you. That's the truth."

"Thank you for saying that." Her voice came out breathless. This was more direct speech than she'd ever heard from him at once.

He held her gaze, his brown eyes serious. "I made a mistake. Letting you go. The way I did it. And I know we can't go back to how we were."

"No. We can't," she said.

Much as she liked this new, truth-telling version of Noah, she'd never let herself trust him again. The next time an emergency came up, he'd be gone in an instant.

"But I don't want to say goodbye right now."

Her breath froze in her chest. "What are you saying?"

"I think I want you to meet my mom," he blurted out.

She stared at him, speechless.

"The idea just popped into my head. It would be a way I could … share with you some of what's been going on with me. I didn't tell you what was happening before, but now I want you to know. Besides, maybe if she met you, she'd see counselors aren't all bad."

Vanessa's emotional whiplash took another sharp turn. He'd never asked her to meet his family the whole time they'd dated.

"It's a bit late to be asking me this now."

"I know. Maybe it's a bad idea." He scrubbed a hand over his beanie. "You don't owe me anything. But … I want to see you again."

She paused for a long moment, sorting through her feelings. Despite all the bullshit, she wanted to see him again, too. She just couldn't tell if that was her bad judgement with men talking.

"I don't know if it's a good idea." Vanessa's fingers tightened on the stem of the rose. Luckily, the florist had trimmed the thorns.

His expression fell. "I get it. I mean, I haven't exactly kept you in the loop."

"No. You haven't. I haven't heard from you in *ten months*, Noah."

"Yeah. Pretty stupid of me."

Noah's sad, lopsided half smile was doing her in, though. If she gave him a chance to show her more about his life, it would also be giving herself a chance. A chance to prove to herself that not all her relationships ended in flames. Maybe at least one of them could end more softly.

They weren't getting back together. She didn't trust that he'd stick around. But he had come back last night.

"I don't know how to fix this," he said after a moment of silence. He might have been referring to them or to his parents.

She drew in a deep breath. "You can't fix everything. But being honest is a good start. Thank you for coming back at least, and for talking to me."

His expression fell further. "I guess I'll get going, then."

He'd half turned to leave when she opened her mouth and said something she might regret later.

"Okay, I'll meet your mom."

He spun to face her. "You will."

"I'm not sure why I'm agreeing to this. Actually, yes. I do know why I'm agreeing. Because you brought me this flower and you told me the truth. It doesn't fix everything, but we can see each other again."

"Okay." The corner of his mouth quirked up, and his eyes

warmed, transforming his expression. "We can text later to set up a time. I'm gonna turn out of the lot and pull over so you can pass me. Make sure you make it out of the parking lot okay."

"Thank you."

He paused, rubbed a hand over his hat again. "And Vanessa. I liked kissing you again."

Before she had a chance to reply, he'd stomped down the porch steps and across the newly-shoveled parking lot.

She shut the door behind her, waited for him to move his truck, and crossed to her car. In the passenger seat, she touched a hand to her heart, which still raced under her coat. The rose on her passenger seat told her last night had been real, and Valentine's Day still held some kind of magic for her.

Things hadn't been fixed between them, but that didn't stop her heart from wondering what if they could be.

Noah's headlights followed behind her all the way until she turned off onto her street.

Chapter 6

Noah's phone had been buzzing in his pocket for the last half hour, and as soon as he cleared the parking lot of The Well Space, he jabbed the button to answer the call.

"Noah. Thank God you picked up. Are you on the way?" Jessie sounded harried, far from his co-worker's usual calm, laid-back attitude.

"Yeah. Sorry. I got held up by something, but I'll be there."

"You don't want to know how many messages we got overnight," she said. In the background, the phone rang over and over.

"No, I don't." He rubbed a tired hand over his face. "I'll look at everything when I get there, but you better get that call. Be there in twenty."

"See you then."

He'd already texted Silvia last night and told her something had come up at work, and he'd stayed there. It did happen occasionally, and he didn't need her worrying about his location.

He swung into a coffee shop drive through for caffeine before heading onto the on ramp into the morning traffic. Running on low sleep and wearing the same clothes as yesterday was not ideal for a busy day like today, but he never got much rest during storms. At least this coffee was hot, if he could avoid dropping it on his lap.

The mornings after big weather events always brought a tidal wave of broken appliances with them. This morning, no doubt a lot of folks had woken up to frozen pipes, appliances fried by the electricity going off and on, or plain bad timing.

Whenever it was a bad time for something to happen, you could count on it happening.

Highway traffic moved at a crawl, with lanes closed and snow piled high on the shoulders of the road. At least two lanes had been cleared and sanded this morning. He kept one hand on the wheel and steered clear of the edges as the traffic inched forward.

He eyed the dead roses on the seat next to him. Funny how one small action led to a hundred reactions.

Before last night, he'd been going through the motions at work, coming home, and going through the motions of dinner and conversation with Silvia. They'd worked out an uneasy truce, wherein he'd eased up how often he asked her about calling Dad or seeing a therapist, and she'd stopped asking him about his personal life, or lack of one. It had suited them fine for months.

But tonight, he'd go home and tell her there was someone he wanted her to meet. He'd have to be careful about how he phrased it, a fact which made his stomach tighten. He'd have to make it very clear they weren't dating. Which was the truth, because he and Vanessa weren't together.

But also, if he introduced Vanessa to Silvia as an ex, she'd get ideas into her head about them dating again. She'd be delighted if she thought he'd found a girlfriend. So delighted, she'd pack up her things and leave, to give him space. And she didn't have anywhere else to go.

He'd surprised himself with the suggestion they meet, but once the thought formed, it felt right. He'd reconnected with Vanessa last night, and he'd finally been able to tell her the real reason for their breakup.

He'd never shared a lot about his family with her when they'd dated before, because his family had been settled and boring. Nothing ever changed with his parents, and that was a good thing.

Until Silvia had shown up on his doorstep that night, soaked with rain, barely able to take another step after she'd walked a half mile from the bus stop. Her foot had been aggravated for weeks after. She'd lifted her chin, sniffed, and told Noah she needed a place to stay for the night. She'd leave the next day, she'd said, and file for divorce. She still mentioned moving out every other day.

She'd knocked over his world with those words, and he'd been fighting to put the pieces back together ever since. And yeah, he could see now that he'd panicked, and he should have told Vanessa what was going on. Instead, he'd shut down. He'd been through one parental divorce in the past, but somehow he hadn't expected a second one.

It wouldn't fix things between him and Vanessa, that he'd asked her over to meet Silvia. But maybe it would help her understand where he was coming from.

He hadn't realized before how much he'd hurt her. He'd

been too involved in his own hurt and chaos, another way he'd failed her. He hadn't done the bare minimum needed to keep her—communicate and tell her what was happening. So he didn't deserve a second chance.

He fell back into the memory of waking up with her this morning, feeling her slight, soft weight pressing against him. And her mouth. He wanted to live there forever, tasting her lips and smelling the body lotion she wore that filled his head with roses.

He shifted on the bench seat, halfway to hard. A common occurrence when he thought about her.

That's not what this was about, him asking her over. He wouldn't be winning her back anytime soon. He couldn't have her in his life. But he also hadn't been able to say goodbye this morning. His feet had plain refused to walk away, knowing he'd never see her again. Not after that kiss.

Something had sparked back to life in his chest in the last twelve hours. He'd been drowning in quicksand since the day they'd broken up. He hadn't realized she'd been his anchor until she wasn't there.

He pulled into the parking lot of Green Appliance Repair, founded in 1975 by Aaron Green, and now managed by him, Aaron's only son. The shop wasn't much to look at, part of a mid-century shopping center that boasted older vinyl signs over worn brick storefronts. It had a decent size storage area for the inventory of parts they needed to keep in stock, as well as an open work space for appliances they'd hauled away to sell or salvage.

A thick layer of ice covered the concrete lot, and he pulled into his parking space with care. When he entered, the sound of the phone ringing greeted him alongside the bells tied to the glass door. Jessie was nowhere around, so he reached across the front counter and picked it up.

"Green Appliance."

"I need to make an appointment for you all to come fix my washing machine," a woman's voice said, sounding impatient.

"Yes, ma'am. Let me check our availability."

He rounded the counter to check the scheduling app on the desktop monitor, and his stomach dropped at the fully blocked out days.

"So, it looks like our first availability is next Wednesday for a technician to come out," he said. By technician, he meant himself or Jessie, the only two on staff at the moment, other than an admin assistant who did scheduling during normal business hours.

"Next *Wednesday*?" The woman's voice rose in tone. "I can't wait a week with a broken water pipe."

"Ma'am, I am sorry. Have you shut off the water?"

"Of course I did."

"You might try calling Frank's Appliance," he suggested, knowing the other shops in town were as overwhelmed as they were. The only question was how many employees they had, and how many extra hours they were willing to work to earn the money to be had after a storm.

"I've called every place in a ten-mile radius," she said, confirming his suspicions. "I tried you guys first, but I got a busy signal. I used to always be able to get someone to come out the same day from there."

He resisted the urge to thunk his forehead on the countertop, because Jessie had just emerged from the back room. Folks always got same-day appointments when Dad ran the shop, because Dad worked fourteen-hour days and rarely came home for dinner. He'd say he had to take the extra business, because if he didn't, someone else would.

"If you'd like, I can take your number," he offered in his most polite customer voice. "Give you a call if we have a cancellation."

"Fine," she huffed.

After she'd given him the number and hung up, Noah set the phone down carefully.

"Sorry. Had to check in the back if we had a part in stock," Jessie said. "Should've known to bring the phone back there with me."

"Not a problem," he told her.

Jessie wore her usual black jeans and white thermal shirt, which she'd rolled up to reveal her tattooed forearms. Her blue hair, cut short on one side of her head, flopped in long waves over her left eye. She was medium height, but her build was so muscular, a lot of customers called her "sir" if they came in the door while her back was turned, a fact that never ceased to delight her.

"It wouldn't stop ringing for even five seconds this morning." She jerked her head toward the phone, which started ringing again, as if to prove her point.

After another call in which he set up an appointment for next week, Noah dropped the phone back on its stand and heaved out a sigh.

"You got my schedule for today?" he asked.

"Yeah. I pushed it to your calendar a few minutes ago. You should have the updated version now."

"Thanks." He didn't make a move to open his phone and check his calendar app. It would be full, the roads were a mess, and he still hadn't had breakfast. Good thing he kept frozen burritos in the back room fridge.

Jessie folded her arms across her chest and regarded him with a raised, pierced eyebrow. "You look rough, boss."

"Thanks," he muttered.

She liked to call him "boss" as a joke, but he was her boss. He was the only one in charge here. On some days, when everything went to hell, it would be nice to have someone else to help. This wasn't how he'd planned for his career to go, but life had thrown him the shop, and he'd taken it on.

"You didn't sleep well?" she asked.

"Something like that."

With a jab, he opened his calendar, looked at the day's scheduled calls, and headed toward the back room to collect the parts he'd need for today's repairs. Jessie's sneakers squeaked on the concrete floor as she followed him.

"As soon as Alisha gets here to take over the phones, I'm heading out, too," she said. "I've got a full schedule today."

"You can call me if you need me." He snagged a burrito and threw it in the microwave.

When Noah had hired Jessie two years ago, Dad had been plainly skeptical. A woman had never worked at Green Appliance, other than to sit at the front desk. But it wasn't Dad's shop anymore, and two years later, Jessie had convinced the old man she could pull her weight. She could repair any appliance as well as he or Dad could.

She'd had to work twice as hard as a man to prove herself, and on top of that, put up with the bullshit men gave her, when they couldn't believe a woman had showed up to repair their refrigerator. A couple guys had even called him up to ask for a different technician. To which he'd replied, take the help he'd sent or call someplace else.

After loading up his work bag with parts and shoving the burrito in his mouth, he slung the bag over his shoulder, but he'd neglected to zip it shut, and two rolls of electrical tape slid out the top. He chased them as they rolled away across the floor. The burrito fell from his mouth into his bag, and he fished it out with a curse.

At the door, Jessie sized him up, clearly not impressed with his organization skills this morning.

"You gonna get some coffee, or what?"

"Already did." He wasn't in the mood for conversation. He never was, but Jessie didn't seem to mind his two-word sentences.

"Well, you might need some more." She flashed him a crooked smile. "Long day."

"Yeah. Don't remind me."

Twenty minutes later, he had the truck packed and ready to go, and he headed out onto the snowy roads.

* * *

Ten hours later, he pulled into his apartment parking lot and cut the ignition. He gathered up his bag and coffee mug, and stuffed the bouquet of dead roses under his arm. He hadn't been able to bring himself to chuck them in a public trash can, but now he'd have to face Silvia's questions. No way she'd miss him coming in the door with flowers.

She was sitting in the living room watching TV when he opened the door, and she took one look at him and reached for her cane.

"Don't get up on my account," he told her.

She ignored him and used the cane to hoist herself to standing. She brushed a hand down her yellow sweater and swung her dark braid, threaded through with gray, over her shoulder.

"I made some dinner earlier. It will only take a minute to reheat."

"Thanks." It was no use arguing with her, and he was hungry after thirteen house calls and a half-hour lunch break. He was also filthy with dirt, wearing yesterday's clothes, and the ankles of his jeans were wet from how many times he'd trudged through snow drifts today.

"You work too much, like your dad," Silvia called over her shoulder as she made her way to the kitchen.

Her bad foot slowed her down less than it had the last few months, but it still took her longer than usual to get to the fridge and open it. Her foot hadn't healed fast enough for his liking. He opened his phone and punched in a reminder to ask her about her specialist appointment coming up. Later, because he had to pick the right time to bring it up.

The smell of cumin and toasted corn filled the apartment as the food heated, and he followed it to the kitchen.

"You made posole. That's a lot of work." A frown creased his brow as he watched her set a large bowl of steaming soup on the dining table.

"Just in the crock pot. I used cans, too. A long cooking time, but no effort. Not everything has to be work."

She pulled out a chair across from his place and sank into it. "Sit and eat. And tell me what was so bad at work last night that you couldn't make it home. And why you have those flowers."

"Give me a minute." He stalled for time by tossing the flowers in the kitchen trash and washing his hands for too long, before joining her at the table.

She leaned forward on her elbows as soon as he sat across from her, eyes sharp on him.

"Let me guess, you had a date. But then work called at the last minute. Some emergency. Am I right?"

"I didn't have a date." He picked up his spoon and took a bite of the soup. He swallowed the rich broth, tart with lime and chile, and felt his insides loosen for the first time that day.

"That's all you're going to say? Hmm, I will have to keep guessing, then." She rested her chin on a finger, pretending to think. "You bought the flowers for me?"

He coughed around a bite of soup.

"Uh. I'm sorry. I didn't buy them for you."

Her dark eyes crinkled at the corners with amusement. "Someone you like, then. Did she turn you down? I'll have a word with her. You're too good for her, anyway."

"It's not that. Just…" He set down his spoon. "I did buy them for someone, but then I changed my mind. So they sat in my truck all day and died. And I was busy with calls after that, because everyone's pipes froze overnight."

Eyes narrowed, she rapid-fired questions at him. "Who did you buy them for? Why did you change your mind?"

"For a friend. For the holiday."

"Valentine's Day." She made a scoffing sound. "We have our own holiday for that."

He drew in a breath, reaching for strength. He'd grown up celebrating every Jewish holiday, even the small, insignificant ones. It had been Silvia's way of staying connected to her community at home in Mexico.

"I know we do. We have a holiday for everything. But she

likes Valentine's Day."

Silvia pounced on the last sentence. "So it *is* a she."

"Yeah. She's someone I know … someone that …" He squared his shoulders, prepared himself to drop the bomb. "I was wondering if you want to meet her?"

Silvia's eyes widened.

"She's just a friend," he rushed on. "Someone I met at work. Who I thought you might want to meet."

The sentence didn't sit right with him. Vanessa was a lot more than a friend, and it was never a good policy to lie to Silvia. But he also couldn't go into the whole background of their relationship with his mom. And she definitely couldn't find out that the timing of his breakup coincided with her arriving to live with him.

"But you like her." Excitement filled her voice. "You bought her flowers, and now you're bringing her home to meet your mother."

"It's not like that." A hint of desperation crept into his tone, his stomach flip-flopping. He needed to distract her from this very bad train of questioning.

"Actually, she's a counselor," he blurted.

The fire went out of her eyes. "A counselor."

"Yeah. She helps lots of couples with their relationships. She's even starting a podcast about it."

Silvia leaned back, folding her arms across her chest. "I see."

Too late, as usual, he realized it had been the exact wrong thing to say. Now she thought he was bringing a counselor over to talk to her about Dad. Which he wasn't. Though it wouldn't hurt her if she could see that counselors weren't completely useless.

She'd been dead set against talking to anyone about her

problems since she got here. He still didn't even know the full story of what happened the night she left Dad.

"I'm not trying to talk you into anything—"

"I don't need a counselor," she snapped. "I don't need anyone telling me what to do. I know I did the right thing."

She stood from the chair abruptly, grabbing for her cane.

"I get it. And that's not why I asked her over."

She raised a brow at him, waiting for more with her fist tight on the cane handle, but he refused to take the bait and explain his real reasons.

"I'll finish up the dishes while you eat," she told him. "Then go take a shower. You stink."

"Thank you for cooking dinner." He picked up his spoon again as she shuffled away.

She paused at the kitchen doorway, shooting him a meaningful look. "I always enjoy feeding you, even though you're grown now. And I always tell you the truth. You just can't accept it."

She meant the truth about her and Dad's marriage being over. He froze, watching her load the dishwasher through the entryway to the kitchen.

Her marriage to Dad had always seemed so happy, so perfect. Dad would come home from work, and she'd feed him, talk to him about his day. Dad always helped her when her RA flared up, and she helped Dad manage the stress of his life. Partnership was for helping each other through the hard things.

But there must have been some underlying problems, things he hadn't seen. She'd left Aaron suddenly and hadn't spoken to him in the months since then. Sometimes, things held invisible cracks, cracks that widened and spread over time.

He finished his soup in a few quick bites, then took his dish to the sink. Despite what she'd told him to do, he rinsed it and added it to the dishwasher.

He got partway down the hall, turned, and came back to the kitchen, where she was wiping down the counters.

"Would you want to meet her if she wasn't a counselor?" he asked.

She stopped and put her hands on her hips. "Of course. Any friend of yours is a friend of mine."

"Can we forget I said the counselor part, then?"

She drew in a deep breath, her expression weary. "Okay. If you like her well enough for flowers, then I'll meet her. But I don't want to talk about that other stuff."

"Got it."

He escaped down the hall to his room before she could change her mind.

He did like Vanessa well enough for flowers. He liked her enough that ten months ago, he'd put a down payment on a ruby ring at a fancy downtown jeweler, and he hadn't been able to bring himself to go back and get a refund yet.

But liking things didn't mean he'd get to have them. Responsibilities came first and put a damper on everything, like the frost that killed the roses.

Still, after his shower, his heart sped when he saw a text notification from Vanessa on his phone screen.

Vanessa: Would Friday work for me to visit? I could drop by after work.

Noah: Friday would be great. 5:30?

Vanessa: I'll see you then.

Noah: When you come, I'll introduce you as a friend. If you don't mind.

There was a long pause before she answered. She could be taking that statement any number of ways, and as usual, he wasn't very good at explaining himself. They weren't dating, but friends didn't quite describe them, either. Exes who'd spent the night and shared a passionate kiss the next morning was definitely *not* the way to introduce her to Silvia.

A moment later, her reply appeared.

Vanessa: That works for me.

So they were keeping it casual. No mention of the kiss, or the fact that she'd slept holding onto his sleeve last night. But she was coming over. He'd see her again, at least one more time, which was more than he'd had twenty-four hours ago.

He passed out holding his phone to his chest.

Chapter 7

Ron and Emily sat on opposite ends of Vanessa's pink couch, looking casual on the surface, her in a beige tracksuit and expensive sneakers, him in designer jeans and a button down. An undercurrent of discomfort hovered between them, though, maybe because they were about to be recorded. Ron folded his arms across his chest, and Emily's fingers smoothed the leg of her pants over and over.

Vanessa gave both of them a warm smile, trying to project confidence. "Thank you so much for coming to my first podcast taping. I hope it'll be fun and painless."

"I'm sure you won't ask the hard questions today," Ron said.

"Absolutely. This isn't a therapy session," she reassured them. "As your former therapist, I know the details about your relationship, but the purpose of the podcast is to share strategies that could help any couple work through a conflict. It's meant to be more general advice."

"I'm not sure what advice I have to give, but we're thrilled you invited us." Emily smoothed a hand down her layered bob.

She smiled at Vanessa, before flicking a more guarded look at her husband.

Something was up between them. They'd had words today, maybe even in the car on the way here. But this wasn't the time to probe into it. They had a podcast to tape.

Fixing a pleasant expression on her face, she turned her laptop around so they could see the screen.

"Let me explain how this works. I'll press record in a minute, and after that, I'll ask you a short series of questions. Answer them as honestly as possible, but only share what you feel comfortable with. This is different from counseling, and we won't dig into your personal problems here. It goes without saying, you can stop at any time. The mic on the coffee table should pick up both your voices, so just speak at a normal volume. We can edit out anything you don't want to keep, so don't be worried about saying the wrong thing."

"Good to know we can edit out the bad stuff my wife's prone to saying." Ron winked conspiratorially at Vanessa. Emily's expression tightened.

"I'm sure you'll both do great," she said, keeping her voice upbeat. "You're going to help so many other couples."

As long as everyone remembered they were recording and didn't wander too far off script. But she could edit things out.

"I'd love to help other couples avoid conflict," Emily said, with another sidelong glance at Ron. "I can tell you from personal experience, it's a lot of work to maintain a healthy relationship."

"It definitely is. As we know from our time together in this office. We'll get the hang of this podcast thing together. It's new for me, too." Vanessa tried to inject as much cheerful optimism as possible into her voice.

But even with all her notes and prepared questions, people were unpredictable. No way to know what they'd say until they said it. At least this wasn't a live recording.

"I think we're ready to get started." She turned the laptop back around and hit the record button. The mic's power light went on, and she pulled the list of questions she'd written in her notebook closer to her on the desk.

"Welcome to The Well Relationship, a podcast produced by The Well Space clinic. In this podcast, we aim to answer all your relationship questions, and give you strategies you can use to improve your life as a couple. I'm Vanessa Bernhard, a licensed couples therapist. Today, I have a real couple with me, and they've volunteered to be our first guests. We'll use their first initials. Welcome, R and E."

"Thank you for having us," Emily said.

"Let's get right into the discussion. I'll ask a short series of questions designed to help our listeners with different issues. Each week, we'll cover a different topic, and this week, we're diving right into how couples handle conflict. There's more than one right way to have a fight, but some ways are more healthy than others, am I right?"

Emily's spine went ramrod straight.

"Right," she said.

"I guess we're still learning about that," Ron said, with a broad smile. "This young lady and I have been married for twenty-five years, and we still have the occasional fight."

"Well, one thing I've learned is that calling women 'young lady' might not be considered the most respectful way of addressing them," Emily said tightly, picking a nonexistent piece of lint off her pant leg.

Vanessa's gut clenched, and she reset her pleasant expression.

"Oh, come on, Emily. I mean, E. Sorry. We can edit that out, right?" Ron raised a brow at Vanessa.

"Of course," she reassured them. She hurried along into the next segment.

"Let's move on to the first question. When minor issues come up in your day, like what to have for dinner, for example, what advice would you give to others about how to handle small disagreements?"

A pause followed her question. Vanessa rested her fingers lightly on the edge of the desk, resisting the urge to grip it.

"Well, I've learned I should approach my partner in a non-confrontational way. I should assume he has good intentions," Emily offered.

Vanessa let out a breath. "That's a really good point. A lot of times, when we know someone well, there's a tendency to jump ahead and assume we know what the other person is thinking. So when we come from a place of assuming positive intentions, it sets us up to have a better conversation."

"But the other person doesn't always have good intentions," Ron interjected. "You can't be positive all the time."

He smiled at his wife—his fake smile. The one he used to deflect tension. Emily's posture deflated.

"Well, let's talk about that," Vanessa said. "What would be some next steps in a conversation that didn't seem to be started with positive intentions?"

Emily and Ron went silent. They'd both crossed their arms now, Emily's gaze on the floor and Ron's expression blank.

She'd been so sure she'd crafted the questions in a non-threatening way, and now this conversation had headed off the rails.

Then Ron opened his mouth and derailed it completely.

"Why don't you tell us what you'd do? In your own relationship?" he asked.

"In ... my relationship?"

"I've always wondered about that," he pressed on. "I'm sure you've gotten into your share of fights. I mean, disagreements. What do *you* do when the other person isn't being positive?"

Vanessa's stomach tightened. "I have been in my share of fights. But of course, this isn't about me. No one wants to know about my love life."

An unnatural-sounding laugh burst out of her. If they knew the truth about her love life, they'd run out the door and never come back.

"To tell you the truth, I *have* always been curious." Emily turned wide eyes on her. "I mean, you've helped us through so many problems, I've always assumed you must be great at relationships. I know you're not married. But you must be happy with your partner. Right?"

"There you have it. Two against one," Ron declared, gleeful. He fixed her with a wide, knowing smile. "Tell us all your secrets for handling hard conversations."

"I ... This is not ..." Vanessa cleared her throat. Her pulse raced in her ears, a flush rising up her face.

She *did* know how to handle hard conversations in her own relationships. She'd done it hundreds of times. Just because none of those relationships had lasted longer than six months didn't mean her communication skills were the problem.

But that's how it would look if she said, on air, that she was still single at thirty-five. That she'd had a series of relationships over the last decade, but they'd all ended prematurely. She'd had twelve boyfriends in the last ten years, each of them a different red flag.

She'd approached dating with hope, and yes, with healthy communication habits. It wasn't her fault that each of those men, at some point, let her down with ridiculous predictability. It wasn't her fault.

In all her plans for the podcast, this scenario had never come up. In therapy, the therapist was not the subject. The therapist disappeared, became a sounding board for the patient's needs. It was never about the therapist, or their personal life. Or their lack of one.

But this wasn't therapy. Podcast hosts talked about themselves, too.

She jammed her finger on the pause button for the recording, her pulse racing. "I think we should take a break."

"Ha," Ron said, his expression smug. "She didn't want to answer that one."

"Leave her alone, Ron," Emily said. She turned to Vanessa. "I'm sorry. That was too personal."

"No, no. It's all right. I wasn't expecting the question to come up. I should have, though, shouldn't I? I should have prepared better." She kept her tone light, professional.

"I think I should go back to the drawing board with my questions, and think about what I plan to bring to the conversation. Because I do want to be part of the conversation."

"Does this mean we're done here?" Ron was already standing from the couch.

"Yes. For today. I'm sorry it didn't go as planned."

"At least we'll miss rush hour," he said. He was out of the office in a few steps, leaving Emily gathering her bag and coat.

"We're sorry, Vanessa," Emily repeated. "We'd love to come back and try again. Well, I would." She flicked a glance at the empty hallway.

"Nothing to be sorry for." She gave Emily a smile and a half wave. The older woman rushed out after her husband.

Vanessa shut her office door with a click, dropped back into her chair, and buried her face in her hands.

What had she thought she'd bring to the table of this podcast? What was her value add, to use the horrible term she'd learned from her social media marketing courses.

She'd hoped this podcast would take The Well Space into new territories for a mental health clinic. Ben had written the books that put the clinic at the forefront of mental health practices, and she'd wanted to build on that success, make it more personal, more interactive.

But to do that, she'd have to interact. She'd have to share parts of herself she didn't normally share with clients, much less the listening public. Thousands of people would hear this show.

Would she share about Toby, the ex who'd been running an illegal online gambling ring? Or maybe Leonard, who'd wanted her to be in charge of everything in his life, from managing his checking account to ordering the events on his calendar?

How to talk about a decade of failed relationships and not sound like a failure, was the question. And she was not a failure. She'd had a run of bad luck with men, and up until last year, she'd bounced back and tried again.

Until Noah. She hadn't bounced back after him. Noah had broken her, and she hadn't tried to date again after he'd ghosted her. Because if a relationship that felt so right could be destroyed in an instant, she didn't have much hope for trying again.

She'd seen horrible relationships last for decades, and it didn't seem fair that a good relationship could end on a dime.

She ground the heels of her hands into her eyes as an unbidden memory from her childhood surfaced. Of coming home from school, using her key to unlock her front door, and walking into another of her parents' arguments. They didn't know she was home, and the words they'd hurled at one another …

She snapped her eyes open, forcing herself back to the present. No sense reliving past problems over and over. The way out of past trauma was facing her fears, trying to work for something better, so the mistakes of the past wouldn't be repeated.

She didn't know how much more trying she had in her, where men were concerned.

She was meeting Noah's mom after work today. She'd agreed to it in the glowing haze of having reconnected with him overnight. He'd given her a rose and apologized and kissed her. Reminded her what good kisses felt like.

And she'd thought for one moment that maybe he was the way out of her string of failures. If she let him in again, and by some tiny chance, things worked out for them, then not all of her relationships had failed.

But he'd also said he would introduce her to his mom as a friend. Which they weren't.

"Red flags," she muttered as she stood and shoved her laptop into her bag. "I specialize in red flags."

She could cancel their meeting. But she wouldn't. She'd go, and see how she felt.

Then she'd go home, order takeout, and take a bath. Try to forget an entire day of awkward conversations.

Noah's apartment was a quick ten-minute drive from the clinic, and memories flashed in front of her as she made the trip. She'd come to his apartment after work on a lot of days, back when they'd been dating. He'd always had dinner ready, a glass of white wine to hand her when she walked in the door. He'd made a point to get home before her to cook. His schedule allowed him to choose his hours, and he'd said he wanted to be around for her.

Those were the little details that had made her sure he was the one, in the short three months they'd been together. He'd thought of those things and done them without asking. He'd been the perfect partner.

Until he hadn't felt like he could share his family crisis with her. He'd only been perfect as long as things were going well, but at the first sign of trouble, he'd ghosted her. Still, he'd come back to the clinic. And he'd invited her here now.

She pulled into a parking space in front of his apartment and cut the ignition. Time to put on a pleasant face, the one she used to meet new clients. Her calm, ready-for-anything expression.

She rang the bell, because of course she'd mailed back Noah's key after they'd broken up. A mezuzah had been added to the door frame since she'd last been here, the tiny scroll encased in filigreed silver.

Slow footsteps made their way to the door. Not Noah's footsteps. His mom, then. She smoothed a nervous hand down her coat and waited while she approached and slid the chain off the door.

The woman who opened the door was of medium height and build, dressed in skinny blue jeans and a tunic sweater the color of pumpkins. She carried a cane, her foot encased in a cast and covered by a black boot. Her medium brown skin was so smooth, it gave no clue to her age. She might have been forty-five or sixty-five. A long, black braid, threaded through with silver, draped over her shoulder. Her brown eyes were sharp as they scanned Vanessa.

It seemed like she was on her own for introductions.

"I'm Vanessa." She stuck out a hand.

"Silvia." The woman clasped her fingers with the hand not holding the cane, her touch warm and dry. She gave Vanessa another assessing look before turning to walk inside.

"Noah, your friend is here," she called into the apartment. "Better put your pants on."

Chapter 8

Noah scrambled out of the shower and tugged on jeans and a T-shirt. This was not how this meeting was supposed to go. He'd planned to answer the door, let Vanessa in, and introduce her to Silvia, so he could watch both women's reactions. They weren't supposed to meet without him, and God only knew what Silvia was telling Vanessa right now. Probably embarrassing stories about his childhood.

He'd taken one extra call at the end of the day, and then he'd been late getting home, late getting a shower, and now this. He took a quick comb to his wet hair and slapped open the door to his room, pulling on his second sock as he walked.

He stopped at the entrance to the living room. Vanessa perched alone on the edge of the couch, her bag next to her on the cushion.

"Vanessa. Hey."

At her name, she glanced up, and his breath stopped. He'd missed seeing her here, in his space. She wore a silky pink top and dark red velvet pants, so she must have come straight from work. She was a tiny colorful hummingbird in his gray apartment, a bird he desperately wanted to keep, but had no idea how to make it happen.

She used to feel at home here. But right now she clearly felt on edge, looking like she'd rather be anywhere else.

Silvia emerged from the kitchen carrying a glass of water, and Vanessa jumped from her seat.

"I can get that—"

"No need. I'm fine." Silvia's tone was firm, and Vanessa dropped back onto the couch, looking uncertain. She couldn't know how prickly Silvia was about accepting help.

Silvia set down the water glass on the coffee table and went to her recliner, where she sat and folded her arms across her abdomen. She seemed relaxed, but not inclined to say anything to make their guest more comfortable.

Noah crossed the room and sat next to Vanessa. "Sorry I was late getting home. I was supposed to get the door when you got here."

"We introduced ourselves," Silvia said, the corner of her mouth turning up. "My son wanted me to meet you, and I said any friend of his, I'm happy to meet."

Now he'd need to steer this conversation toward neutral topics, so Vanessa could get to know Silvia. He'd invited Vanessa here to make her feel like a part of his life, or at least, to show her what his life had become over the last few months.

And maybe Silvia would see that counselors were normal people, and not so bad to talk to. But under no circumstances would he bring up Vanessa's profession.

This would be like walking a tightrope. He should have made snacks to break the tension.

"Well." He cleared his throat. "Since I'm here now, I should introduce you again. Silvia, this is my friend Vanessa."

The word "friend" stuck in his throat, harder to get out than he'd thought it would be.

"And you two met at work? I'd love to hear the story." Silvia rested her elbows on the armrests, leaning forward.

His stomach tightened, because already this conversation was headed in a dangerous direction.

"I called him out to repair the dishwasher at our clinic," Vanessa said with a friendly smile. "We ended up talking afterward."

They'd talked for a half hour, an unheard of length of time for Noah, after which she'd asked him out, then slipped her card into his pocket, her hand brushing his waistband. Good thing she'd omitted that part of the story.

He'd left The Well Space that day with electricity zipping up his spine, her card burning a spot in his back pocket. He hadn't even lasted until dinnertime before texting her.

"Oh? What did you talk about?" Silvia asked. "Noah doesn't always make conversation very well."

He winced internally. She made him sound like a three year-old who didn't play well with others.

"We have a lot of things in common," Vanessa said. "I collect antiques, and Noah's good at fixing things. That's how we started talking. He noticed my roll top desk drawer was stuck half open, and he offered to replace the track on it."

Silvia sat back in her chair. "Ah. Well, he is good at fixing things. He was always ripping everything apart and putting it back together as a child."

"I can see him doing that," Vanessa said, her expression warming. "Anyway, when I saw his full name on the invoice, I

83

asked if he's Jewish, and that ended up being another thing we have in common."

"He didn't tell me that." Silvia narrowed her eyes at him. "You didn't tell me she was Jewish."

"I guess I forgot to say that part," he said.

This was bad. He could almost see the wheels turning in her head. If Silvia hadn't been mentally planning his wedding before, she was now.

"You leave out too much information," Silvia said. She turned to Vanessa. "He's a good man, but he's quiet. Doesn't share a lot about himself. He won the high school science fair three times, did he tell you?"

Noah cleared his throat, a flush rising to his face. "I'm sure she doesn't care about that."

Vanessa turned to him, her eyes sparkling with humor, clearly delighted to hear more about his childhood. "No, he didn't tell me. And I do care. That's pretty amazing."

"Yes, it was very impressive." Silvia's voice warmed as she started in on her favorite subject. "He wanted to be an engineer when he grew up. When he was younger, I used to take him to the pawn shop downtown, and we'd pick out a broken radio or a phone, one of the old ones. What's it called? With the dial?"

"Rotary," he said automatically.

"Rotary phone, yes. Anyway, he'd sit under the table and spend hours taking it apart and putting it back together with his father's toolkit. Until I bought him his own tools."

"I can picture him doing that," Vanessa said, a soft smile on her face.

"He spent more time under that table than out of it. He'd come out for cookies, or dinner, though."

Vanessa cocked her head to the side. "Why did he like to sit under the table? Was it like a play fort?"

Noah's stomach dropped further, because Silvia would be more than happy to answer questions about his childhood all evening. This conversation had gone in a direction he should have been able to predict. But he never managed to figure these things out until too late.

Silvia drew in a breath. "Well, when I first met Noah, he lived under the dining room table all the time. Even slept there at night. He had a big blanket draped over one side, so it was dark under there. His father would slide dinner under the table, and twenty minutes later, an empty plate would pop out."

"Wow, that's quite a story." Vanessa leaned forward, listening with her whole body.

Silvia nodded. "We had a rough start. But later, I got better at figuring out how to make him come out."

"Okay." Noah's voice came out too loud in the small space. "We don't need to bore Vanessa with my whole childhood."

"I'm not bored." Vanessa propped her elbow on her knees. "I think this is really interesting."

"I like your friend," Silvia told Noah. "She pays attention to details."

"She does," he agreed. Better than anyone he'd ever met.

"Well, that's my job," Vanessa said. She said it jokingly, but Silvia froze in her chair, her spine going rigid.

"I'm sure it is part of your job." Silvia shifted her weight to the front of the recliner, gripping her cane and preparing to stand.

She turned her gaze on Vanessa. "Noah wanted me to meet you so I'd be convinced to try going to a counselor. He's so sure if I talk to someone, that will fix everything. As we've been discussing, my son loves to fix things."

She heaved herself out of the chair, leaning on the cane for support.

"Silvia—" he began.

"I'm not as good at fixing things as you are," she interrupted him, sounding weary. "And maybe I don't want to try. I'll leave you two so you can have some time alone."

"We don't need time alone—"

"You don't have to do that." Vanessa spoke at the same time as he did.

Silvia waved them off with a hand. "I'm tired anyway. Vanessa, it was very nice to meet you. I'm going to take a rest and Noah will make dinner. He's a good cook, you know. He learned how from me."

Vanessa opened her mouth, then shut it, unable to agree without giving away their former relationship.

They watched Silvia make her way to her bedroom and shut the door behind her with a click.

"I'm sorry," he said, turning to Vanessa. Her eyes held that sad, world-weary expression, the one that used to make an appearance when she'd come home from work and needed a hug. But they weren't on hugging terms right now.

"For what?" she asked.

"That didn't go like I planned. I thought she'd meet you, have a normal conversation, and see you were a real person. And I thought you'd get a picture of what my life is like now."

A half smile curled the corner of her mouth. "I think I did get that picture. I'm sorry she felt like she had to leave. But I'm glad I met her. I can tell she loves you so much."

"Too much," he grumbled.

She tilted her head to the side. "Noah, can I ask you something? About what she said?"

"Sure."

"She talked about how you were when she first met you. She's not your birth mom, I'm guessing?"

He clasped his hands together and looked down at his sock feet. "She's my stepmom. The woman who gave birth to me walked out on us when I was nine. Dad met Silvia a year later, on a business trip to Mexico. I call her my mom, though. I mean, to her face, I call her Silvia, because that's what she wants to be called. But she's my mom in all the real ways."

"Ah." Vanessa processed that information. "And your birth mom leaving—did that have anything to do with why you wouldn't come out from the table?"

"Yeah." The word gusted out of him. No point in hiding things from her, because Vanessa saw through everything anyway.

"I wasn't … in very good shape when Silvia met me. I was so rude to her at first. Wouldn't look at her or talk to her at all. My plan was to stay in my hiding place and not talk to anyone until I was old enough to move out on my own. I was going to be so self-sufficient." He snorted a laugh.

"You didn't want to need anyone else. Because you'd been let down."

"Something like that. Anyway, Silvia got me out of there in less than a month. First, she'd crawl under the table with a plate of conchas from one of the Mexican bakeries downtown, and I was always starving. I grew fast, pretty early."

"Food is good for bonding."

"It must have worked. I bonded with her hard." He leaned back on the couch, looking out the sliding glass door at the sunset. "She didn't spoil me. Except with food. Other than that, she was strict. The day she got me to come out, she told me, 'Your dad says you want to be an engineer. You want that, you'd better practice.' Then she dragged half of Dad's tools into the living room and let me go at it. Dad had a fit when he got home, 'til he realized I was out."

"She sounds like a great mom."

"She saved my life. I owe her. I'd do anything for her."

"What happened to her foot? If you don't mind me asking."

"She has RA. Rheumatoid arthritis. Her bones break easily and don't heal fast. She gets around, but she needs help. Not that she'll admit it. I had a hard time convincing her to stay here with me. Every other day, she threatens to leave. God knows where she'd go, though. Or if she could take care of everything without help."

His chest tightened at the familiar worry. She could go back to Mexico, for starters. She'd go, and he'd never see her again. He was thirty-two, and still terrified of losing his mom.

Vanessa's brows went down. "I think … I think I judged this situation wrong. This is not what I thought."

"What do you mean?"

"I didn't know any of that background info about your family. I can see a bit better why you panicked. I still wish you would have told me what was happening, though."

"Me too. Having you here tonight … I'm glad you know my situation better now."

"Thank you for letting me come by." She patted his arm, stood, and picked up her bag. "I'll get going now."

He jumped up from the couch with her.

"Will I see you again?" The words burst out of him, the most important thing to know.

"I don't know." She gripped the handle of her bag, looking conflicted. "I came here thinking I should be open minded, see how I felt. That meeting your mom would give me a chance to get to know this part of your life better. And now that I have, I see how important Silvia is to you. And I also don't know if I trust you not to do the same thing you did before. Ghost me at the first sign of trouble."

She took the few steps to the front door and panic threaded through him. She was leaving now, and he wouldn't have a reason to see her again.

"I don't know how to convince you that I wouldn't ghost you again. I don't even know what I'm asking you for right now." He shoved a hand through his hair.

She cocked her head to the side. "What do you want, Noah? Do you want us to get back together again? Is that why you asked me here?"

Noah glanced reflexively over his shoulder. Silvia had the hearing of a cat. When he turned back around, Vanessa raised a brow at him.

"You can't even tell her we were dating," she said.

"She doesn't need to know yet. If she found out, she'd leave."

Vanessa shut her eyes for a moment, pulling in a deep breath. "I'd say call me when you've got it sorted out, but it's already been the better part of a year, and you're still in the middle of it. Maybe you really can't deal with this at the same time as a relationship."

Her hand went to the doorknob.

"Wait," he said. "You asked me what I want. If I thought I had a chance in hell, I'd say I want to try again with you. I want … whatever we can have. If you want to talk more, I'll talk. About myself, about us."

Talking was about the most terrifying thing he'd ever offered to do for her. But he'd do it, if it brought her back into his life.

He'd seen her two times this week, and he was desperate for more.

Her eyebrows flew up. "You want to talk more. You."

He swallowed. "Yeah, I want to talk."

She paused in the doorway, gears clearly whirring in her brain. "You're right there's a lot we didn't discuss. A lot of things I didn't know about you. Coming here tonight showed me that. I was sitting on your couch wondering how many other things I don't know. What else you never told me."

"You said it hurt you. That I didn't tell you things about myself. I'll tell you anything you want to know."

He held her gaze, so she'd know he meant it. Vanessa wanted to know why people did things, their inner motivations. She wouldn't turn down an opportunity to ask him more questions.

She pulled her bag tight against her chest and squared her shoulders. "All right. Come over after dinner tonight. My place at nine."

"Tonight," he repeated. Sooner than he'd expected, but he'd take whatever he could get. "I'll be there."

She tilted her head toward the hallway, indicating Silvia's room. "Make something nice for her dinner. She deserves it."

Chapter 9

Vanessa peeked out the blinds of her apartment window, checking for Noah's truck headlights. Her emotions were playing tug of war with her today, as she swung between the embarrassment of her work day disaster, to the shock of the revelations about Noah that had come from meeting his mom. Between the doubts she'd felt about him, and the stubborn, tiny thread of hope that her heart wanted to weave through the whole thing.

This afternoon's podcast taping had left her raw, forcing her to think about her string of exes in the context of her life as a therapist. Then she'd gone to Noah's house and had her world further turned on its head. Seeing Noah with Silvia made her question everything.

Maybe he wasn't a red flag. And if Noah wasn't a red flag, then maybe not all her relationships had been total failures. She might have chosen well, for once in her life.

She'd assumed he'd cheated on her when he ghosted her. But cheating was the exact opposite of what a man like Noah would do. He was too devoted to the people he loved. He'd given almost a year of his life to take care of his mom, and his relationship with Silvia was a lot more than what she had with her own parents.

She took the bath she'd promised herself earlier, and ordered the takeout, too. Normally, she'd head to bed with a book right now, and read until far too late. Instead, she was waiting for her ex-boyfriend to show up.

So they could talk some more. And if she was honest with herself, his solid, comforting presence was just what she needed after today.

She didn't entirely trust him yet, but she still wanted to see him. He'd said he wanted to try again with her. Whether her heart could let go enough to let that happen was another matter.

The doorbell rang, and she jumped off the couch to answer it. Noah stood on her porch, in his beanie, jeans, and canvas coat, breath coming out in plumes. His gaze raked over her.

She'd changed into her pajamas after her bath, a pink satin set, because she'd wanted to relax. She should've gotten dressed again, made this less casual. Answering the door in loungewear gave the impression she felt more comfortable with this than she did.

"Come on in." She took a step back, and he walked past her into her living room.

Her apartment was cluttered on a good day, and it felt even more crowded with him standing in the middle of it, hands shoved in his pockets. She lived for antique shops and estate sales, and always seemed to come home with one more oil painting, one more piece of jewelry. She loved collecting things that were part of people's personal histories, finding out their stories.

They hadn't spent much time at her place when they'd dated. She'd used her smaller bed as an excuse. The truth was, she'd rarely let a man spend much time here. It had always felt too personal.

"Do you want a beer?" she asked.

He cleared his throat. "Yeah. That'd be good."

She went to the small kitchen and pulled open her refrigerator, the one he'd tuned up to be more efficient last year. She pulled out two bottles of stout and joined him in the living room, where he sat on the edge of her white and gold damask-print antique couch. He took up more than half the space on the delicate piece.

"Thanks." He accepted the beer and took a long swallow before setting it on the table in front of him. He rubbed nervous hands over his thighs. He'd removed his coat and slung it over the back of the couch, leaving him in his usual flannel.

He was so different from the other guys she'd dated in the past. Not a suit-wearing, office job type. He was also quieter, with less of an ego on him than a lot of guys. And his broad chest and thick thighs weren't exactly a turnoff. She pulled her gaze up to his face to find him already looking at her.

His eyes couldn't seem to stay on her face, flicking down to her chest, then at the space past her left ear. He picked up the beer and drained half of it.

"So," he said.

"So."

"We were going to talk. About me, I guess."

"About us," she said. "Though to be honest, I'm not sure why I said yes to this. It's been a day." She took a long swig of her own beer.

His brows lowered. "What happened?"

"Bad day at work. I taped my first podcast episode, and it pretty much tanked in the first few minutes. I had to stop the recording."

"Why'd you stop?"

She drew in a breath. Even though he wasn't her boyfriend, she'd missed this. Having someone patient and calm to tell about her day.

"My clients asked me some personal questions, and I realized I had no idea how to answer them without sounding like I'm completely unqualified for my job. I kind of froze up and ended the session early."

He tilted his head to the side, looking confused. "What do you mean, unqualified? You're the most qualified person I've ever met."

She gave him a small smile. "Thanks. But I'm also a couples counselor with a string of failed relationships. I started this podcast with the idea I could help other people avoid my mistakes. But it backfired on me, because I wasn't ready to talk about them."

"I guess you think I'm one of your mistakes." He twisted his beer bottle around, looking down at his hands.

"To be honest, I did think that. Up until today. Then I wasn't sure anymore."

His eyes, clear and soft brown like a doe's, lifted to meet hers. "You changed your mind?"

"I'm reconsidering. I meant what I said at your place, though. I'm really not sure."

He shifted around, looking uncomfortable. "What would it take to make you sure?"

"That's the part I can't figure out. All I knew was I still wanted to see you again. I took that and went with it."

The corner of his mouth twisted up. "I didn't want to say goodbye, either. I don't even know how I did it the first time."

She leaned forward, the therapist in her taking the wheel. "Tell me what you were feeling that night. When you texted me back and said it was over. I know how I felt, but at the time, I had no idea what you were going through. It seemed like you didn't care at all."

He snorted a laugh. "That's what it seemed like, huh?"

He paused and met her gaze, his eyes stormy with emotion. "It killed me to break up with you. I could barely type the text, my hands were shaking so bad. I couldn't think of any other way. I panicked. I thought I didn't deserve you anymore, since I'd already messed up so bad. But as soon as I sent it, I felt wrong. But I shut it down. I guess I tried not to feel those things."

"Hiding under a table again?" she asked. Her heart raced, but she kept her tone light.

"Something like that."

"Thank you for telling me. I guess … I'm glad to know it wasn't easy for you, either."

"It wasn't."

She tilted her head to the side. "Can I ask you something else about you? On a different topic?"

"Anything."

"Did you really want to be an engineer? You never said so before."

"I did. My degree is in engineering, and I'd planned to be a civil engineer after college. Then Dad wanted to retire, and …"

"And you took over your dad's business. But was that what

you wanted?"

He shrugged. "Doesn't matter what I wanted. It was the right thing to do at the time."

"Right. The right thing to do."

She'd never met someone so dedicated to doing the right thing by his family. Almost to the point of erasing himself. But he'd also shared that information with her now, where before he'd been a blank slate.

He'd let her in, showed her about his family and his past in a way he never had while they'd been dating. She could share some new things with him, too.

She drew in a breath. "You know. Part of why I wanted to talk to you more tonight was seeing how you are with your mom. You have a lot better relationship with her than I'll ever have with my parents. And that's not something to take lightly."

"You never talked much about your parents," he said.

"That's because I don't talk to them. We don't stay in touch. They love me, but … My childhood was not ideal."

"You can tell me about it. If you want to."

"My parents fought all the time. I mean screaming matches, obscenities, throwing objects at the wall. Really loud and angry. They never hit each other, but my home was not … a peaceful place. I used to hide in my room and cover my head with all the blankets, to drown them out and try to sleep."

"That was where your nightmare came from."

"Yeah. They fought a lot at night. When I'd gone to bed, they thought I couldn't hear. Of course, I heard everything. Kids always do." She cleared her throat, which had tightened with the memory. "And their fighting didn't leave them a lot of time and energy for taking care of me, you know? I wasn't the priority. Feeding their own conflict was."

Noah's fingers clenched into a fist on his thigh, but he let her go on.

"Anyway. When I was in grad school, I had a whole intervention with them. I was so sure if they worked on their relationship, things could get better for them. I sat them down and told them I thought their marriage needed serious help, and I knew some great resources to point them to."

He shook his head. "Let me guess. They didn't take that very well."

"No. They told me not to talk to them again until I changed my attitude. They said grad school had turned me against them, and I thought I was better than them now. After that, I never went back home again. We do exchange holiday cards, but I haven't spoken to them in years."

"I'm sorry."

She gave him a soft smile. "You say that a lot around me."

"I'm sorry. I don't know what else to say." He set down his beer, hesitated for a moment, then reached for her hand. His fingers hovered before landing softly on top of hers, curling down between her fingers. He'd always been twice as warm as her.

"So do you have anything of theirs?" he asked. "Photo albums or something to help you remember? I know you like that stuff."

He'd remembered her love of trinkets and antiques, but now he knew part of the reason why. Objects held powerful memories.

"I have a few photos. And some of my dad's vinyl albums he gave me when I was in college. And one of my mom's jewelry boxes. She used to collect them. But it's a puzzle box, and I've never been able to open it."

He sat up straighter. "I could open it for you."

"I know you could. But I think there's a part of me that doesn't want to know what's inside. Maybe there's something amazing in there, like one of her old necklaces, or a love note. But maybe there's nothing."

"Fair enough. If you ever change your mind ..."

"I'll let you know." She disengaged their hands and stood. This would be a good point to end their conversation, but she wasn't ready for him to go yet. They hadn't decided anything, and they were both tired after a long day. And yet ...

"Do you want another beer?" she asked. "Maybe we could watch a show?"

His gaze shot to hers. "You want me to stay? Just to hang out?"

"I think maybe I do." She gave him a small smile. "Don't worry, I won't ask you any more hard questions tonight."

"Then yeah, I'd take another beer."

A half hour later, they were settled on the couch, watching a reality baking show with a blanket draped over both of them, like the other night in her office. She curled closer into Noah's side, an old habit from before. He'd always been so warm, and she fit under his arm perfectly.

His body heat plus the buzz from two beers relaxed her after what had been, all in all, a pretty bad day. If she could have this, come home to him at the end of the day, she'd have all she ever wanted.

The chances of that happening were close to zero. Things had never worked out for her in this department yet.

Still, he was here with her now. So very warm and safe. She pressed further into his side, and his arm around her gave her a squeeze. She felt good with him around. Relaxed, and also more than a little turned on by his smell and the feel of the flannel against her cheek. She slid a hand across his chest and felt his sudden inhale.

"Vanessa."

"Hmm."

"What are you doing?" He tensed under her, as her hand wandered across his pecs with increasing purpose.

He'd always liked it when she was in charge, when she took the initiative and showed him how much she wanted him. He seemed surprised by it every time, though how a man who looked like him could be surprised women wanted him was beyond her.

He was perfect, strong and solid under her fingers. Her hand dropped to his lap, where an impressive erection tented his jeans. Delightful. Under the blanket, she stroked the length of it.

He hissed in a breath through his teeth.

"How long have you been like this," she murmured.

"Since you sat down next to me. You know I can't—" He broke off on a groan as she continued her massage. Not for nothing had she read every sex manual published in the last two decades.

"You're always so hard for me."

"Always." His head fell back on the cushion. "But you should stop. We haven't talked about this."

"I don't want to talk anymore."

She straddled his lap, and it was like scaling a small mountain. His hands came up to help her automatically, and she pressed her mouth to his before he could protest again.

This was what she'd been missing. The feel of his lips and the softness of his beard under her fingers. His taste and his familiar smell of detergent and engine oil, with the hint of the beers he'd drunk.

He was so good at kissing. The best. His breath came faster as she played his responses, the ones she remembered too well. He'd always been helpless against her in this one way, and she reveled in it.

She settled her weight back onto his thighs and reached for his zipper.

"Wait." His hand landed on top of hers. His chest heaved like he'd been running, but his grip held her wrist still. "Wait a second."

"You don't want to?" She nipped at his chin with her teeth, and his head went back.

"You know I do. But you're tipsy."

"I had two beers."

"Two beers is a lot more for you than it is for me."

He was right about that, but her brain was a haze of wanting right now, and she didn't want to think about it. She dropped her face into his neck, inhaled.

"But I missed this."

"I missed it, too." His hands smoothed up and down her back, somehow soothing her nerves and making her hotter at the same time. How did he do that? Make her feel safe and secure, and also ready to rip his clothes off?

"I'll do that thing you like." Her hand squeezed him, where he still held it trapped against his body.

Carefully, he slid her arm up until her hand rested on his chest.

"I do like that thing." He kissed her fingertips. "I like anything you want to do with me. But not drunk. And not when we're not … When we haven't …"

Chapter 9

She slid off his lap, his words draining the warmth out of her. "Right. We're not really together."

She'd almost fallen into bed with a man who hadn't committed to her, something she'd done more than once in the past.

But he reached across the couch and took her hand, and she let him.

"Vanessa. Could we be together again? Is that even possible?" He sounded so uncertain. Like it was an equation he had no idea how to solve, when it was his own life.

Welcome to the club.

"You want to try again," she said.

His Adam's apple bobbed. "I think I do. I think I have to try. If you want that, too. I can't walk out that door and not see you again."

"What about Silvia? If things blow up with your parents, will you bolt again? I don't know if I'll ever feel sure of you."

He shut his eyes for a moment. "Things won't blow up again. And I'll handle it if they do. I'll help Silvia figure out what she needs, and I'll do the same for you."

He paused, an uncertain expression on his face. "But maybe we could wait a while to tell her? See how things go. I want to give her some space, before I bring my personal life into things."

Vanessa rubbed her fingers over her temples, trying to clear her alcohol-fuzzy brain. Keeping their relationship a secret from Silvia was not a good plan. But something had been tickling the back of her mind all afternoon, ever since she'd left Noah's apartment. The pleading tone in his voice brought it to the forefront now.

She looked up at him as the thought coalesced. "I just realized something."

"What's that?"

"You don't want Silvia to leave you like your birth mom left you. That's why it's so hard for you to let go of her."

He was silent for a moment. "You're right. That's why I panicked when she came to me."

"So you ghosted me because you were freaked out. And you freaked out because you'd been hurt in the past."

"That's pretty much it."

"Therefore, you're not a red flag." She stood and swayed in place. Noah's hands reached out to steady her.

"Not a red flag, huh?" His teeth flashed.

She took his face between her hands, threading her fingers into his beard. "Maybe even a green flag. Noah, I think I have a weakness where you're concerned."

"That makes two of us."

"So I will try again with you. But I don't want this to be a secret for long."

"It won't be. I swear." He stood and pulled her into his arms, tight to his chest. "God, Vanessa. I can't believe you said yes."

She buried her nose in his chest. "Me neither. Maybe two beers *was* too much."

"I'm going to make this all work. I swear."

She tipped her head up to look at him. At the man who'd shown back up in her life to confuse her and throw her off, and make her want him so, so much.

He might not make it all work, and he might let her down again. But the part of her that refused to give up on love had flickered to life again in her chest. There was a chance this could work, and her stupid heart would take it.

Chapter 10

Two days later, Noah stood at the loading doors behind Green Appliance Repair, guiding Jessie as she backed up her truck to the rear doors. She'd loaded the trailer with two broken vending machines from a local community center. The old monstrosities were finicky work to fix. He'd have to test the function of each of the individual coils that held products.

Finicky work was fine for today. The flood of emergency calls following the storm had slowed, and he had space to breathe for an afternoon, get his thoughts in order.

He'd promised Vanessa he could make this work, being with her and handling his family at the same time. Too bad no progress had been made with Silvia and Dad in ten months.

He'd been lost in a cloud of idealism that night. Idealism mixed with a healthy dose of lust. And he might have made a promise he had no idea how to make good on.

Almost every day, Silvia made some comment about wanting to move out, which would in theory help his situation with

Vanessa. If he had his place to himself again, he could work on getting their relationship back on track.

But Silvia didn't have any money, and her foot refused to heal fast enough. If she went back to Dad, he'd feel comfortable she had what she needed. But she wouldn't talk about that possibility, for reasons she wouldn't tell him about, either. There wasn't anywhere else for her to go right now.

He didn't want her to feel pressured to leave if he told her about dating Vanessa. And she would feel pressured. So it made sense to hold off on telling her right now.

He rubbed the center of his chest. Heartburn had set up shop there the past few days and hadn't let up. He didn't like keeping Vanessa a secret. She wasn't something to hide. Relationships were so much harder to fix than anything else.

He'd forgotten the delicate clutter of Vanessa's apartment, all those antique lamps and tiny boxes she kept on every surface. The scented candles must have messed with his brain chemistry, because he'd stayed too long, kissed her back when she kissed him, because he couldn't not do it. They'd have done more if he hadn't stopped her.

But she didn't deserve a drunken makeout session from a man who couldn't even tell his family about her. He hadn't known until last night about her childhood, or her broken relationship with her parents. Like the trinkets in her apartment, her emotions were delicate, too easily broken.

He hadn't known any of that when he'd broken up with her. Hadn't realized how easy it was to hurt her.

Jessie threw the truck into park and hopped out of the cab. Together, they threaded nylon straps under the first vending machine and hoisted its edge onto a dolly.

"This one's a wreck, boss," she said, flipping a wave of blue

104

hair out of her eyes. "It's gotta be from the 1970s, latest."

"It does look old."

"I bet it even had cigarettes in it at one point."

He snorted. "Maybe so."

She planted her hands on her hips. "I don't know why they want it repaired. They should junk it and get a new one."

Noah heaved the weight of the machine backward and rolled the dolly down the ramp, while Jessie steered his progress from the front.

He set the machine down in the repair area with a grunt. "Not everyone wants new things. Some people prefer to keep fixing the old."

She slapped a hand on the side of the machine. "I get it if the thing is ten years old. But pushing fifty?"

"You know what they say. They don't make 'em like they used to."

"That's my boy," a voice called out from the doorway. "I trained you right."

Noah's head whipped around. "Dad."

Aaron Green's weathered face creased in a smile. He wore khaki golf pants and a pullover sweater, his usual post-retirement outfit. He'd spent more hours golfing the last two years than the rest of his life combined, and he deserved that break, he really did.

"Thought I'd stop by and see how things were going." He strode over and clapped Noah on the shoulder, pulling him into a one-armed hug. "Looks like you'll have your hands full with these."

Noah resisted the urge to say his hands had been a lot more full the past week, with the storm fallout. Dad didn't enjoy complainers, and besides, he'd known what he was in for when he took over the shop. When Dad retired, he'd made sure Noah knew the expectations of business ownership. Somehow, knowing was different from experiencing the pressures firsthand, though.

"I don't mind. It's a challenge," he said.

Dad stepped back and surveyed the shop. "Good, good. And Jessie's here today, too."

"Yep." The old man said something equivalent every time he stopped by the shop, as if surprised to see Jessie still here. She worked every day, the same long hours he did.

"Good to see you, Aaron," she said with a smile. "How's retirement treating you?"

"Oh, you know. Too much sunshine. Too much free time." He gave her a wink. "I'm glad you're here to help Noah keep the ship steady."

"Of course. Always happy to help," she said, her tone good-natured.

Noah frowned, because Jessie didn't just help. She did half the work.

"Do you want help unloading the other machine from the trailer?" Jessie asked him. "Or I can leave you two to catch up."

"I'll help him with it," Dad said. "You probably have a lot of desk work to catch up on anyway."

"Sure thing." She gave a little wave and headed through the door to the front desk.

"She's a good egg," Dad said when she was out of earshot.

"She is. I wouldn't be able to manage without her. And she doesn't only do desk work. You know that."

"Of course. Sure." The old man sounded distracted, and he ran a hand over his smooth silver hair. "And, uh. How are things going with your mother?"

106

Noah's stomach dropped, because of course this was why Dad had come by today. He'd almost never stopped by the shop in the first year of his retirement, but since Silvia moved out, he'd shown up here once a month at least. To check in on the shop, he said.

"She's doing good," he said. "Still wearing that damn boot."

Dad's brows flew up. "Still? Does she have a follow-up appointment soon?"

"Yeah. I'm taking her next week. The doctor said the bone hadn't healed all the way last time."

"Damn. That's almost a year now."

"You don't have to remind me. Help me unload this?" He gestured to the other vending machine loaded in the back of the trailer.

"Of course."

Together, they shifted the second machine onto the dolly, and Noah rolled it toward the open doorway. He set it down next to the first machine with care, then went to close the doors to the loading area. When he came back, Dad stood with his hands on his hips, trying to look casual and failing.

"And she's … Is she getting around okay?" he asked. He had light blue eyes that crinkled when he laughed, but right now they were shadowed with worry.

"She walks around the apartment. Cooks dinner sometimes, but most nights, she lets me do it. She still gets tired easily."

"That part's normal. She's always had less energy. I used to make sure she—" He cut himself off, shook his head.

That was the thing with Dad. He'd taken such good care of Silvia all those years. Even though he'd worked long hours away from home, he made sure she had what she needed. When she needed a specialist PT, he'd worked extra hours to pay for it. When she couldn't clean the house with her broken foot, he'd hired a cleaner. And worked extra hours to pay for it.

Noah pinned the old man with a look. "She wants to get her own place, she says."

Dad's eyebrows flew up. "What? No, that's … She can't do that."

"I've talked her out of it so far."

"Don't let her. You know she can't." The old man's voice took on an edge.

Noah pulled off his beanie, ran a hand through his hair. "Well, maybe she could, but it wouldn't be the easy choice, that's for sure."

The last couple months, he'd started to question Dad's talk about Silvia not being able to take care of herself. He'd seen her around the apartment long enough to know she could do all the basics. When he pictured her on her own, he worried about her, but she wasn't incapable of pulling it off.

"Son, I … I'm sorry you're in the middle of this. But I appreciate your help."

"Did you try to call her again?"

"You know I have. Once a week since she left. She won't talk to me."

Noah heaved out a sigh. "Yeah, I've asked her to pick up when you call, but she won't."

"Stubborn," Dad said.

"I know it. Guess it helped her deal with you all those years."

When the old man stayed silent, Noah cleared his throat. Communication was hard, but Vanessa had taught him that sometimes, you could make progress with it.

"What were you guys fighting about when she left? She still won't tell me."

Neither of his parents had been very forthcoming about their conflicts. He'd thought their marriage was perfect, but he'd thought wrong.

The old man shoved his hands in his pockets and stared at the ground, then surprised him by answering.

"She said she needed space from me. That I took her for granted. She said I got to come home from work and enjoy the benefits of our home, but I didn't see the work it took to keep it running."

"You did spend a lot of hours working." He tried to keep his tone as neutral as possible.

"I had to. I had to keep this place going. You know what it takes now." Dad kicked at the concrete flooring with his golf sneaker. "And she was fine with it all those years. Or so I thought. Then as soon as I retired, all these issues came up. Not while I was working, but when I finally had free time."

"Maybe it was there all the time, under the surface, and then it came out more when you were home together."

Dad's eyebrows shot up in surprise. "Where'd you get that from?"

"What do you mean?"

"You sounded like our marriage counselor for a minute."

"You guys saw a counselor?" Noah couldn't keep the surprise out of his voice. "She's been refusing to see one since she moved in. I've asked her a bunch of times."

"Yeah, we saw a counselor for the last few months before she left. Not a very good counselor, I'd say. She wanted me to listen to all Silvia's complaints, and I wasn't allowed to say anything back. I had to listen without judgement, whatever that means."

"Huh." Probably would have been good for the old man.

"Then this counselor would talk about our different love languages. What a crock," he added. "By the end of it, we were more convinced we weren't right for each other, instead of things getting better."

"You *are* right for each other." The words burst out of him, a bit too loud. "You guys had a great marriage."

They'd been his model for what love should look like. But maybe something that seemed perfect on the outside could have flaws beneath the surface.

"I thought we had a good marriage, too," Dad said, looking sad. "But I guess even twenty-two years isn't enough to be sure of anything."

"I wish she'd talk to you. I'll keep trying to help, if I can."

"I know you will. You're a good son."

"But ..." Noah paused, chose his words with care. "Do you think there's some truth in what she said? Could you listen to her about what she thinks is wrong?"

The old man's expression hardened. "She's probably told you an earful. Got you on her side."

"It's not like that. I told you she doesn't tell me much. I think she doesn't want to involve me, though I'm pretty involved, with her in my spare bedroom for almost a year."

Dad folded his arms across his chest. "I did what I had to do to take care of the family. I won't apologize for that. I don't need to hear her complaints now, about how she didn't want to be doing her part the whole time."

The man was too set in his ways. Maybe people couldn't change after a certain age.

"I don't think that's what she meant," he said.

Dad tossed up his hands in exasperation. "I've got to get going. If she's still saying all this stuff, nothing has changed."

He paused, a hint of worry creasing his brow. "But ... keep an eye on her, okay?"

Noah blew out a breath. "Of course."

"You need some cash? I still get her medical bills at the house, but the groceries—"

"It's fine. We're doing fine, Dad."

"Okay, then. I'll talk to you soon."

Noah watched his dad make his way down the hallway, wave to Jessie, and exit the front door. His old man was stubborn and old-fashioned.

Also, he must be eating frozen dinners every night. He couldn't be happy without Silvia. But he'd never come out and admit it.

Silvia's point of view was starting to make more sense. She'd been the one to take care of the house, and she'd been the one to raise Aaron's son while he worked twelve- and fourteen-hour days, six days a week. Neither of his parents had had it easy, but Silvia's work had gone unacknowledged for years, while Dad got all the credit for taking care of the family.

Before he could think better of it, he pulled out his phone and texted her.

Noah: I think I get it now. Why you don't want to talk to him.

She replied immediately.

Silvia: Did you see him? What did he tell you?

Noah: What you fought about. I'm sorry I kept telling you to talk to him without listening to your side.

Three dots appeared and disappeared on his phone screen. She typed for a long time. A few minutes later, her reply appeared.

Silvia: I'll talk to a counselor. Maybe your friend can recommend someone.

Shock and relief washed through him. Maybe this situation could still be fixed, and maybe the answer was simpler than he'd thought.

Noah: Why did you change your mind?

Silvia: Because you listened. Maybe it's a good thing to have someone listen.

Noah: It is. And thank you.

Silvia: Go eat your lunch.

He shoved the phone back in his pocket, a mix of nerves and anticipation swirling through his veins. This could be a good thing, though Silvia seeing a counselor didn't guarantee her marriage would be fixed. Still, she'd changed her mind a fraction.

Dad and Silvia's relationship hadn't been perfect after all. Dad had made his work the priority, and this was the result. He had his golf games, and a big empty house to come home to at night.

And Noah had done the same thing to Vanessa when he'd ghosted her. When he'd stopped texting her back, he'd basically told her she wasn't a priority. Even now, he was still asking her to keep their relationship a secret. He wasn't doing much better than Dad.

The weight Dad had asked Silvia to carry—his rude, sullen son, the work of maintaining the house—she'd done those things without complaint. He had no doubt his mom loved him. But when she hadn't been given anything in return, she'd burnt out.

Vanessa would do the same. She wouldn't stand to be kept a secret for long. She'd dump him this time, and she'd be right to do it.

His stomach tightened further. He had to show her how important she was, prove it to her, not with words, but actions. He hadn't made her a priority a year ago, but he would.

He had no model for how to demonstrate to a woman you were all in. But he could fix this.

He ripped into the guts of the vending machine. Some old things were worth fixing, rather than replacing. And he'd never given up on fixing something just because it was hard.

Chapter 11

"Two against one. Tell us all your secrets." Ron's smug voice played over Vanessa's bluetooth speaker for the dozenth time.

She hit the pause button and held her pen poised over her new notebook, the one with faux-fur cherries on the front, forcing herself to listen. A new notebook always invoked positive feelings and made her more likely to get work done.

My personal tips for positive communication, she'd scrawled at the top of the page in her messy handwriting. She had a hundred pieces of advice she'd give clients on the tip of her pen. But connecting those things to her personal experiences was new.

The podcast was as much about her, the host, as it was about the interviewees. How vulnerable she could make herself on air was up for debate, though. Maybe she could give away some details about her relationships without revealing the whole truth. She could draw out lessons from her experiences without sharing embarrassing secrets. It would be a fine line, though.

She tossed her pen down and shoved her chair away from the desk. The next podcast taping was in less than a week, and she'd have to have some material ready. But for now, her page remained blank. So much for the lure of a new notebook.

A shadow passed her doorway, and she jumped up. Anything for a distraction. Cameron's back retreated down the hallway, and she followed him, taking two steps for every one of his.

"Cam, is that you?"

He stopped and turned, a guilty look on his face.

"What are you doing here?" she asked. "It's only day four of your vacation. I'm not supposed to see you here for another three days."

He held up his hands in a gesture of surrender. "Would you believe me if I said the wifi at home is terrible? Because that's true."

"It might be true, but you're still not supposed to be working. Don't you have a jigsaw puzzle at home? A book?"

"I have lots of books. Books for my research."

He looked worse than the last time she'd seen him, the dark circles under his eyes more pronounced. He looked like he hadn't slept in a week.

"Do you want to chat for a minute?" She tilted her head in the direction of her office door. "I have tea."

"Fine." His shoulders sagged. "But just for a few minutes. I have more to get done tonight."

Back in her office, she boiled water on the kettle, poured it over a teabag, and handed him the mug. He'd slouched his long frame into one of her smaller chairs, which somehow only made him look taller. The top two buttons of his shirt were unbuttoned, his suspenders of the day plaid.

"So. Back at work during your vacation." She scanned his face, looking for clues about what might be going on. He'd always been a hard worker, but this was a new level, even for him.

He scrubbed a hand over his face. "Don't tell Ben. He said I can't be here at all during my time off."

She gave him a reassuring smile. "I won't. I got you this job, so it's not like I want to get you fired. But I wish you'd tell me what's going on."

She'd met Cameron when he was a brand new grad student and she'd led a seminar for one of his classes. After her lecture, he'd introduced himself to her, cited her own Master's thesis to her, and told her he admired her research. When a job opening at the clinic had come up, she'd recommended him. He'd been a stellar admin assistant for Ben. But right now, he was a mess.

He drained half his tea and set the mug down on the table. "My wifi at home does suck. I wasn't lying about that."

"Okay." She paused, giving him time.

"I just … I don't think I can afford to slow down right now. This is the worst time for me to take a break, but Ben said I have to. June, maybe. But February? Midterms are next month."

"Midterms are in March. You've got a few weeks."

"There's a reason why spring break is after midterms. Everything before that is fair game to these profs."

"How's the study going?" She switched the subject, trying to find the source of his tension. Cameron was leading a research study on stress in the workplace during his final year in his PhD program.

He gave a short laugh. "It's going horribly, thanks for asking. I have the advisor from hell, whose only purpose in life is to pile more work onto me, in addition to my current workload."

"Is there someone you can talk to about it? A supervisor in the department?"

"He is my supervisor."

"I see." That explained the change in his mood lately. "Well, what are you doing to take care of yourself?"

"You sound like Ben right now. He's all self-care and taking long lunch breaks these days. He didn't care about that stuff when he first hired me."

"He has softened up a bit this year." Ever since Ben had fallen in love and gotten engaged, he'd paid a lot more attention to his staff's well being. He wanted everyone to be as happy as he was. It was nice in its own way, but not everyone appreciated it.

She tried not to smile at Cameron's obvious distress over being made to take lunch breaks. The man hardly noticed he had a physical body. He probably hadn't drunk any water all day, either.

"So your plan is to work straight through your vacation," she said.

"Of course that's my plan. It has to happen, whether it's here or at home."

She tapped a finger on her chin. "I won't tell Ben if you promise me one thing."

"Okay."

"When spring break happens in March, you will take a real break. You don't have to go to Florida or anything. But you'll stop working for a week."

He slugged back the rest of the tea. "Fine. I promise. But this week, I'm gonna be upstairs in the office working. No one even uses the space right now."

With Ben out of the office for his honeymoon, the third floor was empty. That was how Cameron had been sneaking in to work unnoticed.

"It's a deal," she told him.

His eyes focused on her, sharpening in suspicion. "And what are you doing here late again? I've seen your light on every night this week. Should I tell Ben when he gets back?"

He must really be tired if it had taken him this long into their conversation to notice.

"The usual." She kept her tone light. "The damn podcast. And you're welcome to tell Ben. I'm not the one who's supposed to be on vacation right now."

"It's not going well?"

"I'm trying to work more of my personal experiences into it. And I don't like it."

He frowned. "You've got a lot of experience."

"What I've got is ..." She shook her head. "No. I don't want to frame it that way anymore. I was about to say a track record of failure."

Her relationships had not been failures. She'd learned from all of them. She just hadn't seen the red flags until too late.

"Cameron. Can I ask for your opinion? What would you think about a man who wants to keep your relationship a secret from his parents? Are there any circumstances you can think of that would make that okay?"

Cameron leaned back in his chair, brows down, his giant computer-like brain going to work. She could almost see him mentally scanning through the research articles he'd read.

"There aren't a lot of good reasons for doing that. But maybe a couple. If the man's relationship might hurt the parent in some material way. Or if the parent was abusive or toxic, and they'd gone no-contact."

118

"Right." She cleared her throat. "That makes a lot of sense."

"Why do you ask?"

"I've been ... sorting through a lot of my own personal experiences lately. I appreciate your opinions, though, because I don't seem to be very good at being objective about my own life."

"No one is."

She turned on a high-wattage smile. "You're doing great work, did you know that? You're going to be an amazing practitioner."

The corner of Cameron's mouth turned up and some of the tension dropped away from his shoulders. "Yeah. That's the goal. If I make it that far."

"You'll make it. Someday, Ben's gonna hire you as a therapist, and you'll have the office next door to mine. And I'll make you go home at 5:00 every night."

"If I get to that point, I'll do it." He stood and stretched out his long legs. "And now ... I am going home to my sucky wifi and my frozen spring rolls."

"Take care, kiddo. I'm staying to work a bit longer."

After he'd gone, Vanessa sat back in her chair. Of course Cameron was right. There weren't a lot of good reasons to hide a relationship from a parent. Maybe in Noah's mind, he thought telling Silvia about their relationship would hurt her in some way. Or maybe he was still scared, and hadn't changed at all.

As if she'd conjured him, her phone lit up with a text.

Noah: Are you still at work?

Vanessa: How'd you know?

Noah: I'm at your apartment and you're not here.

She pressed a hand to her chest, because her stupid heart had raced into overdrive at the thought of him waiting at home for her. Even with their relationship on uncertain footing, her body hadn't gotten the message that he wasn't hers.

Noah: Can I come to the clinic for a minute? I need to ask you something.

Vanessa: Something you have to ask me in person. What is it?

Noah: I need to say it to your face. OK to come by?

She pressed a thumbs-up onto his message and set the phone down on her desk. He'd be here in ten minutes. Whatever he couldn't tell her in a text meant enough to him that he'd left work, and instead of going home to check on Silvia, he'd gone to her house first.

The beams of his headlights swung into the parking lot, and she made herself walk, not run, downstairs to meet him at the door. It was probably nothing. Except it was something. He wouldn't come here for nothing.

She pulled the door open just as his boots hit the steps. He stood on the porch, looking delicious in his work coat and jeans.

"Can I come in?" he asked.

"Sure." She stepped back to give him space to enter and watched as he toed off his work boots in the foyer, revealing thick wool socks. He shrugged out of his coat, hung it on a peg, and turned to face her.

"You're here alone? Your car's the only one in the lot."

"I'm here alone."

He shook his head. "I don't know how I feel about that. It's not safe. But also, it means I can do this." He reached for her and hauled her into his chest in a tight hug.

Her body melted into his, the tightness in her chest loosening. It couldn't be something bad, if he'd come here to hug her. The flannel was soft and warm against her face, and he held her, hands smoothing up and down her back.

She felt his chest rise as he took a deep inhale, before he pulled back enough to look at her face.

"Sorry. I didn't ask if I could hug you. It's okay?"

"Yes. It's okay with me, Noah."

"Good." His eyes hadn't left hers, his gaze strangely intense. "I came here because I have to ask you something."

"Okay." She tried not to hold her breath.

"Will you go out to dinner with me?"

A laugh bubbled up in her throat, but she suppressed it. He looked too serious right now. "That's what you came here to ask me?"

"I needed to ask you in person. Because I realized something about us. About how we were before."

His hands squeezed her upper arms, slid down her forearms, and grasped both her hands in his, not breaking eye contact.

"What did you realize?"

"I never asked you."

She frowned, confused. "What do you mean?"

"The day we met, you asked me out. Once we'd been dating for a while, you'd ask me if I wanted to go out to dinner that weekend. You'd make all the reservations. After a while, I just assumed you'd come over after work. But I never asked you."

"I ... Maybe you're right."

"So I realized I needed to do that. To ask you this time, if we're going to start dating again. To show you I'm choosing you. That I would choose you again. Every time."

Her eyes burned, throat tightening. The words she hadn't realized she needed to hear hung between them.

The old Noah would never have said that. He'd been hiding this part of himself behind a wall, and now he'd let it down a fraction, and she saw the heart of him. The part that was dedicated to the people he cared about, loyal to a fault. Except now she was now included in the circle, rather than outside of it.

She swallowed. "Thank you. That means a lot. Thank you for coming here to tell me. But ... what brought this on?"

He shook his head, shutting his eyes for a moment. "I talked to both my parents today. It made me realize some things, that's all. And one other good thing came out of it. Silvia said she'd talk to a counselor. She was wondering if you had any suggestions."

Vanessa swiped at her eyes with her sleeve. "I can get some resources together for her. It's great she's willing to try."

It was a step toward Silvia working through her problems, and maybe then Noah wouldn't feel the need to hide his relationship from her. She could try this with him, for a little while. Because of how he was looking at her right now.

He still hadn't released her hands, his expression intense on her face.

"Tomorrow night, I'm coming to pick you up at seven. Okay?"

"Okay."

"I'll take care of the plans. And if you wanted to wear the red dress …"

This time, the laugh did escape her throat. "I have a few of those. But I know which one you mean."

He gave a sharp nod. "Good. It's my favorite. Vanessa, I'm gonna show you this time how important you are to me. I won't mess this up."

Chapter 12

The next night, Vanessa sat on the edge of her sofa in the tiny red strapless dress, the one that cut off her breathing but made her small boobs look fantastic, and checked the time on her phone again.

Noah was a half hour late, and whatever else he'd been while they'd been dating, he'd always been punctual. Something must have come up with work, or at home, and he should have called by now. A simple explanation would be better than silence.

He was thirty minutes late, and inside her head, she was right back where she'd been ten months ago when he refused to answer her texts. She sucked in a breath, restraining herself from texting him.

He'd said he was going to make all this work, which meant he had to be able to handle his family, work, and a relationship at the same time. That was his promise, so he needed to be the one to text her.

She flopped back onto the couch with a huff. Her current level of hotness hadn't been achieved without forty-five minutes of effort, time she could have spent doing something else. She'd give him fifteen more minutes before changing out of the dress.

She swiped across her phone, but the illuminated screen showed no new messages.

Her stomach tightened further, because she'd started to trust him, and this was the result. He was letting her down yet again, which she should have expected—

Her phone buzzed with a text.

Noah: I'm sorry. I was in the ER with Silvia. She's OK, but the last hour was kind of crazy. I didn't get any cell service inside the hospital.

She sat up straight on the couch, grabbing the device.

Vanessa: I'm so sorry to hear that. What happened?

Noah: She fell and the doctors wanted to do a set of X-rays because her bones break easily. But nothing's broken.

Vanessa: I'm really glad she's OK.

Relief flooded her, that Silvia was okay, but also that he'd had a good reason for not texting her. In light of the direction of her thoughts the last hour, she felt ridiculous now. She'd been so quick to jump to the worst conclusions.

A pause followed, the dots of him typing flashing on her screen.

Noah: I know this was supposed to be our night. I was all

dressed and in my truck, ready to go, when it happened.

Vanessa: It's not your fault. Things come up.

It had happened before, and would happen again, especially with his family situation. When would she stop having a bad reaction, afraid he'd ghost her at the next big emergency? He'd said he wouldn't do that again, but some part of her still didn't believe him. The house of her fears had been built too strong, from too many bad experiences in the past, and her poor heart huddled inside, a bird in a cage.

Noah: Let me make it up to you. Saturday afternoon, maybe?

Vanessa: OK. Saturday afternoon. But if you need to cancel, please let me know. That's not too much to ask.

His reply appeared a moment later.

Noah: I won't need to cancel. I'll pick you up at 12:00.

She clicked the phone off and set it down next to her on the couch. They had another date, but something else could come up for him on Saturday. His life was complicated, and she'd never feel certain.

"What a mess," she said out loud to her empty living room.

She went to her room to change into pajamas, draping the velvet dress over the white, wrought-iron chair at her vanity. Two hours ago, she'd sat there and perfected her makeup, thinking of the intent look in Noah's eyes, so different from before. There'd been something new there, and she hadn't imagined it. Too bad real life had a way of intruding on romance.

She sat in the same spot and removed her makeup, wearing the cotton shorts and tank top she slept in. She'd watched her mom do the same a hundred times growing up. Sometimes, Mom would be crying as she sat there, after some fight she and Dad had at dinner or in the car on the way home.

Vanessa had watched her and learned some important lessons. One, that she was never going to let a man treat her like that. And two, that she should get out at the first hint of a relationship going bad.

But it was possible she'd overreacted in the past. That she'd run away from men at the first hint of trouble. Her reaction tonight was a prime example.

Some of the men she'd dated *had* been red flags. But others might not have been. They hadn't been bad men, just complicated people doing their best. Like her. But she'd always bailed before things had a chance to go anywhere.

It was possible, slightly possible, that she had red flag issues of her own.

She went to the kitchen and heated a frozen dinner. After eating it on the couch, she tossed the tray in the trash and went up to bed, where she stared at the ceiling.

Saturday was three days away. Something else might come up, but she would assume, for now, their date would happen. She would choose to believe, and try to silence the voice in her head telling her it might not happen.

The next morning, she came out of the apartment, cradling her second mug of coffee, and stopped in her tracks when she got to her car. A dusting of snow had fallen overnight, but her windows had been scraped clean. And a pink rose had been stuck under the windshield wiper. He must have bought that this morning, because the flower wasn't frozen. He'd have been here in the parking lot before 7:00.

She pulled the rose from her windshield and tucked it into her bag. It was hard to stay worried about the loyalty of a man who did things like this.

He scraped her car the next two mornings. He also salted the path from her door to the parking lot. She knew it was him, because the apartment management never salted, and the path only went from her door to the lot.

A mix of gratitude and guilt filled her as she imagined him coming here before dawn every morning to do those things. She'd been so quick to assume he'd ghosted her again the other night, and now he was bending over backward to show her he was there for her.

He didn't text her again, though. He still wasn't a man of many words.

By the time Saturday rolled around, anticipation thrummed through her, which was ridiculous, because a few days ago, she'd been ready to bolt. But she needed to see him again, to know if the change she'd felt in him a few nights ago was real, or if she'd imagined it.

She'd gone for casual this time, burgundy jeans and a white top with the top two buttons undone to show off the edge of her pink lace bralette. Brown half boots and her vintage round leather handbag.

This time, he knocked on her door right on time, and she opened it to find him standing there, looking far too good. He'd showered recently, and combed his damp hair back from his face. He wore newer-looking blue jeans and a solid blue button-down under a down vest.

"You're not wearing plaid." She gestured to his shirt, saying the first thing that popped into her head.

He looked down at himself. "Oh. Yeah, I guess not. You look great," he said quickly. "I mean, you always look—"

He cut himself off, pinched the bridge of his nose between his fingers. "Let me say something else first. I'm really sorry about the other night."

"You couldn't help it."

"I couldn't. But you're right. I should have texted you and let you know."

She cocked her head to the side. "But you didn't have cell service."

He looked down at his shoes. "I know. But I could have gone outside for a minute—"

"It's okay."

"But it's not. I know exactly what that must have looked like to you."

She pulled in a breath. "I was … worried the same thing was happening. As before."

A pained expression crossed his face. "That's what I didn't want to happen."

"But you have a lot to deal with right now. You told me you were handling everything, and I should have trusted that you were."

His brows lowered. "I could have done better."

She pulled her door shut behind her and threaded her arm through his. "Today will be better. I can already tell."

He walked her to the truck and held her hand to boost her up the step. Inside the cab, she turned to him.

"So where are we going? You said I always planned things before, so I'm curious what you've got up your sleeve today.

Your strangely non-plaid sleeve."

"You don't like my shirt?" He ran a hand down the front of it. "It's still flannel."

"Well, that's a relief. Thought I'd gotten into a truck with the wrong guy for a minute there."

Her heart expanded with the light feeling of teasing him, of being taken someplace by him on a date he'd planned. It didn't matter where they went, because this day already felt different.

The cupholder of his truck held a bottle of sparkling water—her favorite brand. He'd added a heated seat warmer on her side of the cab, too. He was nothing if not detail-oriented. She should let him plan more of their dates.

They headed downtown on the highway, until he pulled off at an exit near the riverfront area. A farmer's market dominated several blocks of the neighborhood in the summer, and in the winter, merchants sold arts and crafts as people shopped for the holidays. This time of year, it was usually deserted, which made her even more curious what he had planned.

"This is our first stop," he told her. "We won't be outside long, I promise." He pulled into a parking space on the street and jumped out of the truck to pay the meter.

After she got out of the truck, he hesitated for a moment before grabbing her hand. His was warm, his fingers enveloping hers. They walked two blocks to the open brick square where the farmer's market stood.

She stopped walking when they rounded the corner. "Food trucks! I had no idea these were here."

"Not just any food trucks. There's one you have to see."

He led her across the square to a purple truck with white lettering on the side, spelling two of the world's most beautiful words: Knishes and Bialys.

She stopped in her tracks. "You brought me to knishes."

"I did." Noah looked pretty proud of himself as they joined the short line of people waiting.

"You know they're my favorite. And no place in town sells them."

"I did recall that." His smile broadened, and he squeezed her hand.

She barely restrained herself from bouncing on her toes as he placed the order for six knishes and three bialys, enough to save extra for later. The paper bag the short, dark-haired woman handed her through the window smelled like pure nostalgia—caramelized onions and potatoes.

Noah grabbed her hand again and led her back to the car.

"Where are we going now? When can we eat these?" she asked, smelling the top of the bag.

He glanced down at her, his expression amused. "You can eat them whenever you want, but I did have a plan."

"Okay. I'm trusting your plan. I will be a pinnacle of strength, and not open this bag."

"Won't be too long. I promise."

He navigated the truck through the one-way downtown streets, until he hit the curving road that ran alongside the river. Ten minutes later, he pulled the truck into an empty lot and parked in a spot facing the shore.

"Now, I know you don't want to eat outside in the cold. So that's why I got the seat heater. But there's a pretty good view here."

She gazed out the windshield over the river's dark water, as it drifted in icy currents between the banks.

"The view is nice. The ice is finally melting off," she said.

"Not the water. Over there." He pointed to a bend in the

131

river and she drew in a sharp inhale.

"Swans."

Several dozen of the big white birds drifted in the calmer water at the bend of the river, silent and graceful.

"I know. They're finding their mates for the season. They got back early, which is cool, even though global warming sucks. They have no clue it's still February. They do these dances around each other this time of year. Anyway, I thought you might like to see them. Because you like to see how people find their mates."

She stared at him for a moment. "I think ... This was a very good idea you had."

He smirked and ducked his head. "Good."

He opened the paper bag and handed her a knish wrapped in waxed paper. She took a huge bite of the warm potato filling wrapped in yeasty dough. She'd never been much of a cook, but she could appreciate good food when it appeared in front of her.

She shut her eyes to appreciate the taste. When she opened them, Noah was looking at her.

"You really like knishes," he said.

"Food of our people. Keeps you alive in the harsh winter." She took another bite, the flavor bringing back memories of eating the pastries with her parents on their occasional trips to bigger cities. She'd had moments of happiness in her childhood, and she held onto them tightly.

"I guess it does. I grew up eating Mexican food, so that's my comfort food. But this is good, too." He added mustard to his own knish and took a bite.

"There they go." He pointed out the windshield toward the swans. A large male circled his mate, their necks bobbing and weaving around one another.

"I wish I knew what they were saying to each other," she said.

"They don't need to talk. This works fine for them."

She swallowed. "I guess it does."

Noah didn't talk much himself, but he seemed to see things other people didn't get.

She'd always been so focused on healthy communication. But a lot of communication happened without speaking. Like the way he cleared off her car. Or the way he couldn't seem to help reaching out to put his hand on her knee in between bites of his lunch.

They watched the swans flap and glide over the frigid water as they polished off the food. Noah ate three knishes and a bialy, and Vanessa managed a second knish before leaning back against the warm seat and patting her belly.

"Well, that was amazing, but I might need a nap now."

Noah put the key in the ignition. "We have another stop."

She turned her head on the seat rest to look at him. "What else have you got planned?"

"Nothing much," he said casually. "Just the antiques fair came to town this week."

Vanessa sat up straight, suddenly awake again. "We're going to look at antiques?"

"Or we can go home if you're tired." The corner of his mouth turned up.

She liked seeing this side of him, the teasing side that was openly delighted he'd pleased her. The side where he got to pick, she let him take them wherever. She hadn't given him many chances to do it, but she'd misjudged him. Noah knew what she liked.

"You had better not take me home right now," she told him.

"We're going antique shopping."

His rich, rare laugh filled the cab. "Okay. Let's go, then."

Chapter 13

He'd made the right choice, bringing Vanessa to the antiques fair. She'd dragged him from one end of the convention center to the other, looking at booths of used and rare books, jewelry, and furniture. They spent a half hour at the appraiser's booth, watching people get estimates for their family heirlooms.

She squeezed his hand as they wove their way between the tables, talking about bringing in her mom's belongings so she could have them appraised, and insisting that no, he didn't have to buy her one more thing.

He had bought her one more thing, though. He'd already purchased a set of seed pearl hairpins to add to her collection, a miniature brass lantern, as well as a bag of cotton candy. And the last item he'd gotten was in a small cardboard box in his pocket.

The afternoon had gone better than expected. Sitting in the ER with Silvia two days ago, he'd been sure Vanessa would never speak to him again. Today was a reprieve, a chance to show her he could do it right. And so far, she'd loved it.

His chest warmed as he watched her down the rest of the cotton candy. He wanted to be the one who brought that satisfied look to her face all the time.

When they got back to the truck after two hours of exploring, she flopped onto the bench seat, exhausted but buzzing with energy.

"I have to come back again tomorrow," she told him, buckling her seatbelt. "I need to make sure I visit that puzzle box vendor one more time. I didn't get a chance to try them all out. And I'll bring in part of my jewelry collection to the appraiser."

"I wish I could take you again tomorrow. But I've got work."

"On a Sunday?" she asked, incredulous.

He shook his head, disgusted with the thought. "It sucks, I know. I don't normally work on the weekends. But we got in a big shipment of parts, and no one had time to do inventory this week."

Vanessa sagged into her seat, some of the excitement seeming to go out of her. They'd had a good date, but one good day didn't fix everything.

"Well, thank you for today. I'd say that was the best date I've ever been on."

"Good." He turned on the ignition to get the heat going, but didn't pull out of the parking space yet. "I had a good time, too."

"Why didn't I let you plan more dates before?" she asked, looking thoughtful.

"You liked to plan things. And I was amazed you wanted me at all. I'd have gone on a date to an alligator farm with you."

She snorted a laugh. "Sounds too muddy. But seriously, that's how you felt? You were surprised I wanted you?"

136

"Of course. I still don't know why."

She drew in a long breath. "That is … I should have told you before. You honestly don't know. Noah, I'm sorry."

He cocked his head to the side. "Sorry?"

Her eyes took on a tinge of sadness. "I'm realizing some things I did wrong in our relationship. You ghosted me, but I wasn't perfect, either. I assumed a lot of things about you."

She pushed her glasses up her nose, straightening in her seat. "So let me be clear now. I wanted you because I felt safe with you from the start. You made me relax, and I felt like I could be myself with you. And also, you're really hot."

He shook his head. "I'm not."

He knew what he looked like. The man who greeted him in the mirror every day was sturdy, a little soft in the middle, and completely average-looking.

"No, you are. I love how big and strong you are. And your beard is super soft, did you know?"

"Stop."

"Especially on my neck. Love that." She gave a mock shiver.

Heat rushed into his face. He needed to change the subject before she put any more images into his head he couldn't do anything about right now, in this crowded parking lot.

"Anyway." He cleared his throat, rubbed his hands on the thighs of his jeans. "I got you one more thing. While you were looking at the jewelry."

He dug in his pocket and pulled out the cardboard box poking him in the leg. He opened the lid to reveal an antique brass keychain with an engraved letter V, surrounded by enameled flowers.

Her expression brightened. "Oh, it's so pretty."

"Yeah." He rummaged around in his other pocket. "It'll work

perfect for your key."

She stopped in the middle of reaching for the box. "My … key?"

He extracted the silver spare key to his apartment and picked up the keychain so he could slide it on the ring.

"Yeah, your key to my place. I'm giving it back to you."

At her silence, he stopped twisting the key onto the ring and looked up at her.

"Oh. Shit. I brought that up wrong."

He'd had the key in his pocket all day, had meant to give it to her right away, but there hadn't been a good time. And then he'd seen the keychain, and it seemed to make sense to get it. She'd need a keychain anyway. But the look on her face told him he'd done it wrong.

It *was* kind of a big thing, giving someone a key to your place. And he'd assumed she'd want it back, but she didn't, did she? It was too much, too soon.

"Okay," she said slowly. "I don't want to jump to any conclusions. Can you tell me why you're giving me back my key right now?"

He set the key, now on the keychain, on the seat between them and withdrew his hand as if the thing had burned him. She didn't pick it up.

"I, uh. God, I'm bad at this. To tell you the truth, I didn't realize how this might look. I wanted you to have it back so you could come over whenever you want. No." He shoved a frustrated hand through his hair. "No, that's not the whole reason."

She continued watching him, her eyes round, but she didn't interrupt. He could say the rest, put into words what he'd been thinking when he'd put the key in his pocket this morning.

"The reason I want you to have it back is because I want you back. All the way back in my life, however we can make it work. Not sort of dating, or trying it out. I don't want to keep you on the back burner. I want you to feel free to come to my place whenever you want. I don't want you to worry if it's a good time. It's always a good time for me to see you. I just … I want you to know you're important to me."

Her jaw had dropped open through that speech, probably more words in a row than he'd ever said to her.

She seemed shocked into silence, so he kept talking to fill it up.

"Anyway. You don't have to take it back right now. I just realized it's too much, too soon. I know that now, and I—"

The breath rushed out of him as she flung herself at him, launching herself into his lap.

"I want it back. Noah, I do want it."

She crushed her mouth down onto his, and his arms tightened around her, pulling her slight, warm weight against him. She tasted like cotton candy and her mint lip gloss, and all his thoughts melted away under her onslaught, except damn, he must have said something right in all that mix of words.

The key pressed into the back of his neck. She'd scooped it up at some point during his speech, and she had it clutched tight in her fist as her lips moved over his, her other hand threading into his hair. She made a sound of frustration and slung a leg over his, straddling him. He pulled her higher against him, head falling against the headrest as she kissed the life out of him.

A catcall from outside the window forced him to pull his lips away from hers. They were still in the middle of a very crowded convention center parking lot.

She pressed her forehead against his, breathing fast. "Take me home now. Please."

"Yeah. Okay, I can do that."

"And you're making love to me when we get there. Just so we're clear. If you want to."

"I want to. God, Vanessa." It was a thirty minute drive. He might not survive it. Not when she was looking at him like he hung the moon, like he was everything she'd ever wanted.

How he'd thought he could live without this, he didn't know. He'd been the biggest idiot alive to break up with her, and she'd somehow, miraculously, given him a second chance.

Breaking the speed limit would get them stopped, though. Traffic crawled as they inched out of the parking lot in the long line of cars. Her hand slid onto his thigh, rubbing a few inches higher.

He was ragingly hard in his jeans, had been ever since her lips touched his, and this must be how he died. Expired from unrequited lust in a traffic jam, while the love of his life leaned closer to him, pressing her breasts against his arm.

And she was his love. The only one who'd ever seen past his quiet front, past his inability to say what he meant, and seen what was in his heart. And she seemed to want him too. Still. Again.

He peeled out of the parking lot and onto the highway. Vanessa's fingers wandered up his torso, unbuttoned his top button, and slid inside. He had more than an average amount of chest hair, which she inexplicably seemed to like. She slid her fingers through it, and his heart rate ratcheted up another notch.

This was far more wound up than he'd ever been with her, and that was saying something. She'd always known how to drive him crazy, but this feeling was different. Visions of picking her up and tossing her down on the truck seat consumed his brain. He could see himself doing it, throwing the truck into park and to hell with anyone who might see.

Then she had to go and unbutton two more buttons on her shirt. She'd had the thing too far open all day, flashing him the pink lace underneath that he'd tried so hard to ignore. But now the shirt gaped open, revealing the inner slopes of her breasts, the curves milk-white and dusted with freckles.

It was a red flag in front of a bull. His vision hazed, and he stomped on the accelerator. Five minutes until they were home, and then …

"You're awfully quiet, there." She traced her fingertips down the curve of one breast and pinched her nipple. A quiet gasp came out of her, and her head fell back against the seat.

"You have to stop. I can't—"

"Can't focus?" she asked, her tone teasing. "Well, I do want you to drive safely. You keep your eyes on the road, and I'll get started on this by myself."

Her fingers undid the rest of the buttons and the front of her shirt fell open. The groan that escaped him didn't sound like him, but he wasn't himself right now. He'd fallen into a pit of lust, and he didn't recognize the person who spoke.

"You'd better not," he growled.

"Better not what? This?" She ran her hands down her torso, parting the shirt all the way and lifting her chest for his inspection.

He slammed his eyes shut, then forced them open and onto the road. Two more minutes.

He screeched into the parking lot of her apartment, killed the ignition, and jabbed an index finger at her.

"Stay."

He marched around the side of the truck, lightheaded from all the blood in his body having drained south. He popped open the passenger door and hauled her out, pressing her front against his chest so none of her neighbors could see her naked to the waist.

A surprised squeak came out of her at the action. He'd never manhandled her before, despite having a hundred pounds and over a foot in height on her. She'd always been so independent, and he'd let her lead the way.

But he was not in his right mind at the moment. He marched her to her front door and dropped her on her feet in front of it.

"Unlock it," he demanded.

Her hand fumbled the key as he dropped his face and sucked a bite into her neck. Her skin was delicious, and he was starved for this, like he hadn't eaten for months.

"Let me just …" The key wouldn't quite make its way into the lock. Her hand shook too badly.

"You said you like this. My beard on your neck."

He sucked the spot again, then bit lightly, his hands flattening against her abdomen and pulling her hips back against him. She hissed in a breath when she felt his erection pressing against her.

"Yeah. You did that to me." He spoke the words into the crook of her neck.

Finally, her door fell open, and he nudged her inside. As soon as it swung shut behind them, he scooped her up again, carrying her like a bride through her apartment. A shocked sound came out of her, halfway between a moan and a sigh. Her eyes were dark pools, the pupils all the way dilated.

"You like me carrying you," he told her.

"I … think I do."

"This is what you need." He'd never seen it before, because she'd always been so capable, so skilled. She knew every sex position in the book, and she'd tried a lot of them out on him. She'd always been in the lead, and he'd been happy to let her. But today, she needed him to be in charge, to take care of her.

He strode into her bedroom, considered the frilly, too-small bed, then pivoted and plopped her on her antique oak dresser. The ancient piece looked sturdy enough.

"What are you—"

He stopped her question with a kiss, felt her melt against him, and his brain whited out to pure static.

His hands tore open the button on her jeans and yanked them down, lifting her hips up so he could work them down her legs. He extracted one of her ankles, then abandoned them, too impatient to remove them all the way. They dangled from her other ankle as he ran his hands over her arch, up her leg.

His hands looked like paws against her delicate skin. He pushed her offensive shirt off her shoulders and sucked her breast into his mouth through the lace of her bra. She cried out, arching her back.

He worked her over with his mouth, hands pulling her tight against his torso until she was grinding against him, seeking relief.

"I didn't see it before." He dropped to his knees in front of her, pulled her underwear aside, and swiped his tongue against her sex. Her sharp inhale filled the tiny room. "What we did before, it wasn't what you needed. Or not everything you needed."

"Oh my God." Her head fell back on her shoulders, and she

braced her arms behind her on the dresser as he took her apart with his mouth. He already knew what she liked, every inch of her familiar to his mouth and tongue.

But this time was different because this time, he was doing the taking. She needed this from him, and he would give it to her.

By the time she fell apart under his mouth, thrashing against him, his hands were shaking, his heart a thundering pulse in his head, his cock.

He stood and undid his jeans, found the condom in his wallet, and rolled it on. She'd curled over, resting her head on his chest, her breath going fast and her muscles limp. He nudged her thighs apart again and stepped between them.

"You only get this from me. I'm the only one who knows what you want." He notched his erection between her legs and pushed inside in one long stroke. Finally. Electric pleasure flooded his system.

"Only you." Her head tipped back and she looked up at him, eyes huge and mouth slack with pleasure.

He grabbed her thighs, hiked them against his ribcage, and unleashed himself on her.

Everything he'd felt in the last year—losing her, losing the one thing he'd wanted the most in the world, then getting her back—he poured into this one perfect fuck. His body tried to pound its way inside her, and her head fell back again, her hips rising to meet him. He felt her clench around him, coming again.

All of it was so perfect, the top of his head threatened to explode. He'd never been harder, and the coming orgasm was a huge one, scary in its intensity. The bright edge of it rose in front of him, then he was gone, shouting his release into her hair.

Spots danced in his vision, and he fought to slow his breath, make his legs more steady. A few breaths later, he withdrew, gathered Vanessa's pliant body against him, and laid her out on the bed. He found a tissue and got rid of the condom before returning to her.

She was lying in the same position he'd left her in a moment ago, her eyes shut and her arm above her head, bent at the elbow. He bent to remove her jeans from her ankle.

He hadn't even taken her panties off. She still wore those, her shirt, and her bra. She was so beautiful, there were no words.

And maybe that had been too much for her.

"I'm sorry. That was—"

"Don't you say sorry." She didn't open her eyes.

"It wasn't … too rough?"

Her eyes popped open, and she held out an arm to him. "Come here."

He knelt on the edge of the bed and lowered himself beside her. She curled into his side and draped an arm around his middle.

"Noah Green. I don't know what just happened, but I loved it."

"Yeah?" A smile curled the corner of his mouth.

"Yep. You're going to stay here a while longer with me. Maybe take a nap. And then, we might think of a few other things to do."

She was back to taking charge, calling the shots. But that was okay, because she'd let him in. She'd let him take care of her. And she had his key again.

Warmth spread in his chest, stealing through him like a drug.

He shut his eyes and let himself drift.

Chapter 14

"She's not going to get here any sooner, the more times you check."

Silvia's voice startled Noah, and he dropped the living room blinds. So maybe he'd checked the parking lot more than once for Vanessa's car.

He'd left Vanessa's house on Saturday in a haze of satisfaction, and he'd had to suppress the giant smile that wanted to stretch his face as he came in the front door. Silvia was too observant, and everything he did or said could give him away.

All he had to do was stay quiet today while Vanessa talked to Silvia, something he was usually good at. Vanessa had gathered some counseling resources, and she'd offer those to Silvia and answer her questions.

They'd also decided not to tell Silvia about their relationship today. Vanessa had told him they should focus on the counseling resources and not drop any big news on Silvia yet. Maybe later, they'd agreed.

But he didn't want to stay quiet about Vanessa anymore.

He wanted to tell anyone who'd listen that the most amazing woman in the world was somehow, inexplicably his again.

Ten months ago, he'd been so panicked about his parents' relationship that he'd torpedoed his own. But he had no doubt now that he could keep helping Silvia and date Vanessa at the same time. Vanessa understood him better now, and Silvia would understand, too.

Maybe it would be smarter to wait until Silvia saw a counselor. Maybe Vanessa's information would help Silvia see her way to what she needed to do next. Her problems seemed huge, but there had to be solutions she hadn't thought of yet.

The doorbell rang, and he crossed the room in three strides to open it. Vanessa stood there, wrapped in one of her vintage coats and wearing those pointy, heeled boots that made her maybe five foot two tops, and he wanted to pull her into his arms and kiss her senseless. It had been two days since he'd seen her, and he missed her.

She hadn't used her key, not that he'd expected her to.

"Hey," he told her. His eyes roamed over her, drinking her in. This would be difficult. He was going to spend the next hour pretending this woman was a friend, and his body and his face were trying their best to betray him already.

"Hey, yourself." She smiled up at him, eyes shining behind her glasses.

He cleared his throat. "Come on in."

He hung up her coat, and she took a seat on the sofa.

"Water?" he asked.

"Sure, that sounds good."

As he went to the kitchen, Silvia passed him on her way to the living room. Over the tap running, he heard the sounds of them greeting one another. When he came back, he found both women seated at opposite ends of the couch, looking more friendly than last time, but still polite and distant.

Silvia might still be suspicious of counselors, but she had her head cocked to the side, examining Vanessa as if her opinion might be worthy of actual consideration.

Noah took the recliner, sitting opposite them.

"So," Vanessa said. "Noah said you were interested in finding some resources for couples working through relationship issues."

Silvia nodded slowly. "I told him I'm willing to listen."

"So, I'm not here in a professional capacity. I'm not going to give you relationship advice, but it would help me if I understood the background of what's going on, so I can point you in the right direction. Maybe you can give me a short overview?"

Silvia raised an eyebrow. "The short version is that I left my husband last spring. I haven't spoken to him since. That's the overview." She crossed her arms over her chest.

She'd worn one of her woven tunics today over her jeans, the bright orange and turquoise one with the embroidered edges.

She looked stronger lately, happier, her face less weighted with worry. Her foot was healing up, too, and the boot would come off in a couple of weeks. All these positive changes had happened since she'd been apart from Dad.

"Can I ask how you and Aaron met?" Vanessa asked. "I've been curious about that part."

"At temple," Silvia said.

"Dad had a work conference in Mexico City," Noah explained. "Some of the major appliance manufacturers moved their assembly plants there, and they were supposed to take some tours of the facilities."

Silvia nodded along. "That's right. And while he was in town, he went to services on Friday night."

"You always said it was love at first sight," Noah said, glancing over at her. "At least, that's what you used to say."

Silvia gazed out the window. "I think it was. I still believe love at first sight is possible. I took one look at Aaron, and something inside me clicked. We were married three months later, and I moved here."

"Was it hard, leaving Mexico?" Vanessa asked.

"Very hard. I missed my family, the community there. I grew up speaking Spanish and English, so I didn't have to learn English when I came here. But everything else was so different. I was lonely, more than I'd ever been. I'd always had neighbors and friends around me, and then it was just me."

She wrapped her arms around herself, lost in the memory. "Then I got sick. A couple of years after we got married, I was diagnosed with RA. It didn't stop me from doing anything I wanted to do, but it's gotten worse over time. Of course, Aaron didn't sign up for that when he married me."

"Wait, you think Dad didn't want to take care of you?" Noah asked. "He was happy to take care of you. He loved it."

It had always been one of the things he'd admired most about his parents' marriage.

"Maybe so. In his own way." She let out a sigh. "He made sure I was okay, that I had everything I needed. But he also wasn't around. I had the best medical care. But what I wanted was more time with him. And that wasn't something he could give."

"He worked long hours," Vanessa said.

Silvia nodded. "Of course he did. Owning his own business, he had to. He always told me, when I asked, that he had to take care of the family, take care of me and Noah. He did a good job of that. But my heart didn't always feel it."

"You wanted to feel more connected to him." Vanessa nodded. "That's really common for women in relationships. Men don't always have the communication skills to say what they feel. It doesn't mean they don't return your feelings, though."

Noah stared down at his shoes. If he made eye contact with Vanessa now, he'd give himself away. He knew exactly who she meant with that last statement.

"You might be right." Silvia trained her gaze on Vanessa, considering. "I don't think Aaron ever once had a conversation with me about his feelings. He'd say 'I love you,' but that was it."

Vanessa nodded. "Okay. It sounds like you're dealing with some difficult issues, but nothing too out of the ordinary. I have some recommendations for counselors, and therapy groups, too, if that's something you'd be interested in. They can help with fostering better communication skills. There are support groups for people with RA we could look into as well. I'd recommend a couple of books—"

"Wait." Silvia held up a hand. "I'll take your recommendations and think about them, but I can't promise I'll go to counseling. I don't even know if I want to talk to him again. I've had the opportunity, but I can't answer his calls."

"Why do you think that is?" Vanessa tilted her head to the side, looking curious.

Silvia shifted on her chair, looking uncomfortable for the first time in the conversation. "I worry … that I'd cave the minute I saw him. I do miss him sometimes."

Noah's heart leapt in his chest. She hadn't said this much in the last ten months.

Then she crossed her arms across her chest, her tone turning stubborn again. "But he thinks he knows what's best for me, and he doesn't. I always went along with what he said in the past. But the truth is ..."

She sighed and leaned back in her chair, some of the fight going out of her. "The truth is, I married him so fast, I never had a chance to find out what's best for myself. I quit my first job and left my home for him. He was a decade older than me. He made the money. I raised his child and took care of the house."

She turned to face Noah, her brown eyes warming. "My son. You know I love you."

"I know," he mumbled.

She held his gaze. "But being a mom is a lot of work. Work that no one thanks you for, and no one sees. And I did that work joyfully. You were the best part of my life. But I also got tired. I wanted something for myself, and Aaron didn't understand."

"Mom. I'm sorry." The words squeezed out through the sudden tightness in his throat. He almost never called her that, and at the word, her expression softened further.

On the couch, Vanessa observed them, staying quiet. Therapists were pretty damn powerful, if her simple questions, offered without judgement, could make Silvia talk like this.

Silvia reached over and patted his knee. "Don't be sorry. I'm not sorry about it. But I also needed some space to think. To just be. Away from his house."

"I get that now. I wish ... I wish you could have told me before."

"You didn't ask."

"Thank you for sharing that," Vanessa said. "I think the

152

experience you're describing here is called invisible labor."

"Invisible. That's about right." Silvia raised a brow, considering. Her eyes scanned Vanessa as if seeing her in a new light.

"Lots of women experience this," Vanessa said. "And it's normal for it to create resentment and burnout over time. So don't rush yourself. Given everything you said, it seems best if I leave you with the resources, and you can decide if and when you want to use them. Maybe you'll decide you want to try, but it sounds like maybe you're not ready yet. And that's fine, too. But I might be able to offer you one piece of advice?"

Silvia nodded. "Go on."

"In my experience working with couples, it's common for their long-term patterns to get in the way of them expressing who they are now, who they've become. The couples who make it last long-term are the ones who are still willing to respect their partner as they are now. Not for who they were twenty years ago. I guess I'm saying, if you told Aaron what you just told me and Noah, you'd have a chance at saving your marriage. If you decide it's something you want to save."

"What would you do?" Silvia's voice took on a note of urgency, her eyes pinning Vanessa. She'd never seemed interested in another person's opinion of her marriage, but she wanted to know Vanessa's answer.

"What would I do?" Vanessa echoed. She was silent for a moment before continuing. "I guess I'm a person who keeps on trying, even when love knocks me down. I'll always fight for love."

"Why?" Silvia asked, sounding genuinely curious. "You of all people must know that love doesn't always work out like it does in the movies."

153

"No, it doesn't." Vanessa shook her head, looking deep in thought. "It's messy and even awful sometimes. It can be the worst feeling in the world. But ... it's the reason why we're here, right? Why else are we on earth if not to love someone? If I didn't have that belief, I wouldn't be doing what I'm doing."

Noah's heart thundered in his ears. He wanted to launch himself out of the recliner and pull Vanessa into his arms. He'd knocked her down, pushed her away, and she'd come back to him. Let him back into her life. She let herself be vulnerable to love, over and over.

Silvia nodded, thinking it all over. "You made a good point. And I thank you for your advice."

Coming from Silvia, that was high praise.

"I'll go now," Vanessa said, rising from the couch. "Give you guys time to talk, and I'll text you the information I talked about."

Noah jumped up from his seat to walk her to the door. Under Silvia's watchful eyes, he handed her her coat, opened the door, and waved goodbye to her. Just like a friend. He shut his eyes for a second before closing the door and locking it behind her.

"She's a smart girl," Silvia said when he returned to the living room, her sharp eyes examining him.

"She is."

"You should date her."

Noah choked on his own spit and coughed for a few long seconds. Silvia had never suggested he date an acquaintance. She had to suspect something.

"That's not ..." He started to deny it, then went for the subject change. "You can worry about my love life later. For now, we need to figure out yours."

She lifted her chin. "I have no love life."

He folded his arms over his chest, and she crossed her arms too, mirroring him. "You could again, if you wanted."

"If I wanted. That's the key. I don't know if I want that yet. Even your counselor friend agreed I should take my time."

"Fair enough. Dad is stubborn as hell."

"He is."

"He didn't listen to you."

"He also didn't talk to me," she added.

"How did you guys last twenty-two years?" Noah shook his head in disbelief. "I thought things were so perfect between you guys, but they weren't. I guess it was a mix of good and bad."

She raised an eyebrow at him. "He had a few good points. If you really want to know, he was great in bed. That helped."

"Oh my God. Silvia." His face burned red to the tips of his ears.

She threw her head back and cackled. "I like this communication thing. It makes you uncomfortable."

"I'm going to cook dinner now."

He escaped to the kitchen to think and breathe. The sound of TV drifted through the wall as he pulled out a skillet, potatoes, and onions on autopilot. Tacos de papa were Silvia's favorite comfort food, and he could make the filling in his sleep. They might even be a relative of Vanessa's knishes. He'd have to make them for her sometime.

Nothing had changed, but the talking had cleared the air. Vanessa had brought things into the open that his mom hadn't been able to discuss all year. If she could do that, counseling was closer to magic than he thought.

Vanessa was magic, and perfect, and fragile and strong at the same time. If he could keep her for a little longer, until this all

155

worked out, he'd be the luckiest man.

Chapter 15

The side of Vanessa's face pressed into the cool oak of her dining room table, and she gripped the molded edge, trying to catch her breath after the marathon sex. Noah's torso pressed down on her, a delicious weight against her back.

"Your neck is blushing." He kissed a spot behind her ear, an open-mouthed brush of his lips.

"Mmm." Words were hard to make right now.

A moment later, she felt a hand brush over her hair, almost tender.

"Still can't believe you want it like that." His voice was low in her ear.

Like the last few times, he'd taken charge today, pinning her against the wall as soon as she'd opened the door for him. This new version of Noah was so different, bossy and right on the edge of rough in bed. She hadn't known he had it in him.

She drew in a shaky breath. "Oh, I want it like that. But you might have to help me stand."

He withdrew from her gently, helping her up from the table. As soon as she stood upright, he pulled her against his chest in a tight hug. Then he bent at the knee and slid one arm under her legs, hoisting her up into his arms.

"This still okay?" he asked.

She grinned up at him. "You really like carrying me around."

"Just … let me."

"All right. Only you, though. Everyone else better not try it."

"I know, baby. Just because you're small doesn't mean you're easy to move." He smiled down at her, seemingly unaware of the endearment he'd uttered.

"But you let me do it," he added, sounding satisfied.

She sniffed. "Only because my legs are unsteady right now."

But that wasn't the whole reason. It was kind of nice, being carried. Being taken care of, and letting someone else be in charge. Trusting someone to do the right thing by her.

All of those things had been hard before, with other men, but they were getting easier to do with Noah.

He strode into her bedroom and set her down on the bed, then went to the bathroom to dispose of the condom. He'd come here every night after work this week, knocking on her door and pulling her into his arms.

He'd made love to her on every surface of her apartment, and sometimes even the bed. He seemed to have an unending supply of this energy, this new dynamic where he took over and took care of her.

He knew what she wanted more than she'd known it herself. They'd always had chemistry, but now it was on another level, so hot she couldn't help but want it again and again.

She'd let down her guard around him, much further than she'd let it down when they'd dated before. And nothing bad had happened so far.

And he'd let her into his family life, let her get to know Silvia. He was showing her he could work on his family problems and be with her at the same time, which was more than he'd been able to do before.

He joined her in bed and she curled into his side, her arm resting on his bicep. He was so warm, a giant space heater that kept away her bad dreams. He never stayed overnight, but sometimes he'd lie with her for a couple of hours.

He lifted his head to check the clock on her bedside table before dropping it back on the pillow.

"You need to head home?" she asked.

He'd told Silvia he was working late nights at work this week, an explanation that might not have gone over well with her, considering the problems in her marriage.

"Not yet. We've got some time."

"That's good." She yawned and squeezed him tighter against her.

Too soon, it was time for him to go, and she watched as he pulled on his jeans and T-shirt, then stuck his arms through the sleeves of his flannel. She'd never get tired of watching him, a fact he still didn't seem to understand.

"Is that jewelry box the one you can't open?" he asked, nodding at the dresser as he pulled on his socks.

"Yeah. My mom's puzzle box." She kept it there front and center, for reasons she didn't understand.

"Sure you don't want me to open it for you? I'm sure I can get it."

She sat up in bed, the sheet pooling around her waist. What was she so afraid of finding in that box? It likely held an old pair of earrings or a cheap necklace, nothing of worth or even sentimental value. Except it was all she had of her mom now.

"Okay," she said. "Go ahead and take it with you."

"All right." He picked up the heart-shaped metal box, his hand dwarfing the thing. "I'll take it to the shop and see if I can figure it out. I'll bring it back tomorrow when I get it."

He was so sure of himself, sure he could fix this thing that had been broken or stuck shut for decades. But people didn't always want their broken things fixed. Silvia didn't necessarily want to save her marriage. And she and Noah had barely gotten started again.

A lot could still go wrong. She was trying to believe it wouldn't this time. As often as it popped up, she silenced the voice of doubt that rose in her mind, the one that said every small thing was the beginning of the end.

She'd been too quick to judge in the past. Her own insecurities had more to do with her previous breakups than she'd known. And she'd had good reasons for avoiding getting too close to anyone.

But Noah proved her wrong at every turn. He was reliable, and he understood her need for reassurance a lot better now.

He bent at the waist to drop a soft kiss on her mouth. "I'll text you."

"Okay."

"Get some sleep."

"I'll try." She would sleep some, but it wouldn't be as peaceful as if he stayed here with her.

She heard the click of her front door shutting and got out of bed to lock it behind him. She hadn't given him a key to her place, of course. Because it was still too soon.

* * *

The next afternoon, she sat facing Ron and Emily, hands clasped on her desk.

"Thank you so much for coming back for a second attempt," she told them, keeping her tone light. "I know the first recording session didn't go how any of us expected, but I think this time, I have some better material to start with."

Ron folded his arms and leaned back in his chair. "Okay, young lady. Let's see what you've got."

What she had were some carefully constructed anecdotes about her past relationships, which revealed some interesting issues, but not the whole truth. She could still be in control of this conversation.

This time, she'd set up two chairs right across from her desk, so the three of them sat closer together in a small circle. The mic stood in the center of the desk between them. Up close, she'd be able to see their facial expressions, and also, the closer they sat, the more likely they were to see her as a real person instead of a counselor. She'd be an equal participant in the conversation.

"Okay," she announced. "I'm going to start recording and get us going. Just like last time, remember we can edit things out if needed, so please don't worry about making a mistake."

She pressed the record button and gave the same intro speech she'd used last time, saying the planned words and hoping the rest of the conversation followed suit.

"Welcome to The Well Relationship, a podcast produced by The Well Space clinic. In this podcast, we aim to answer all your relationship questions, and give you strategies you can use to improve your life as a couple. I'm Vanessa Bernhard, a licensed couples therapist. Today I have a real couple with me, and they've volunteered to be our first guests. We'll use their first initials. Welcome, R and E."

"Thank you for having us," Emily said, in the exact same polite tone of voice she'd used in the first recording session. She sat ramrod straight as usual, in black track pants and a designer brand sweatshirt.

"So, we're jumping right into a big topic this week and talking about how couples handle conflict. I thought I'd start by telling you about how some of my own personal experiences have shaped how I handle conflict. That might spark something you connect to, that you want to share with our listeners."

Emily's eyebrows went up, and Ron leaned forward in his chair.

"That sounds good," Emily said.

Yeah, this wasn't how she'd started the podcast last time. But she'd have to open up and share some details of her personal life to make this work, to make her seem relatable. And what was more relatable than having relationship issues like everyone else?

"So, I've had my share of conflicts in relationships, and some of them weren't pretty. I'll give you an example of how I handled it, and feel free to chime in."

Ron nodded, looking far more interested than he ever had in their therapy sessions.

She drew in a deep breath. "Okay. So I had an ex-boyfriend who was addicted to gambling. Now, addiction is a whole separate topic, one we won't have time to cover in today's podcast. But I want to talk about how that led to failures in communication between us."

162

No need to mention that Toby had been arrested a week after their breakup for illegal activities.

"Even when I didn't know what was going on with his personal life, I felt a lack of attention from him. He was physically present, but not really there with me. I chalked it up to stress, or him being absent-minded. But I should have asked him more questions."

"How did you find out about the gambling?" Emily's eyes had gone wide with interest. "Did you snoop on his phone?"

"You mean like you look around in mine?" Ron said, his voice mild, but threaded with irritation.

"Any spouse should be able to look in her partner's phone, if he has nothing to hide," Emily said, clasping her hands around her knee. Her tone was as pleasant as if they were talking about the weather.

Ron stiffened in his chair. "People need their privacy. That's not an unreasonable expectation."

"Let me answer E's question," Vanessa interjected, keeping her voice calm, but firm. "Then I'll get back to your point."

Ron leaned back in his chair, and she turned to Emily. "I found out about the gambling when he opened a credit card in my name and took out ten thousand dollars in loans on it."

Emily and Ron made twin gasps of surprise. Couples often grew to look like one another over their years together, and their shocked expressions matched perfectly.

"Anyway," she continued. "At that point, you can bet we had a conversation about his gambling. Until then, I hadn't put two and two together. So you can see that waiting for a crisis point to start talking is not a good policy."

"That's so terrible," Emily said, jaw slack.

And this was why she hadn't wanted to talk to her clients

about her own relationships. In comparison to her own relationships, their problems didn't seem so bad.

She cleared her throat. "To speak to your comment, R. I agree with you that even people in committed relationships need privacy, and they need their partner to trust them enough to give them that privacy."

"Ha!" Ron exclaimed, triumphant.

She held up her hand. "But. You have to give your partner reasons to trust you. That's earned, not a given."

"See, that's what I've been trying to tell you." Emily turned to her husband. "You haven't earned it. Not lately, anyway. You've flirted with other women—"

"It's not flirting—" Ron's voice rose in uncharacteristic intensity.

"And I have no reason to expect I might not find some other woman's number in your phone," Emily plowed on.

"You'd better stop now," Ron said, his tone sharp. "We're being recorded, young lady."

The hair on Vanessa's neck stood up, because they'd argued in her office plenty of times, but they'd never gotten this close to saying what they really meant. Even though the sharp edge to Ron's tone set her nerves alight, she would let them go on.

"We can talk about this now, if you want to," she said. "But please keep it respectful, and remember I can edit things out later if you prefer."

"Yes, let's talk about it now," Emily said. "I don't care who hears it."

She turned to Vanessa, her expression almost frantic. "He changed his phone passcode. There's something he doesn't want me to see. I want to know what it is, and he won't tell me anything—"

"What I want is for you to stop assuming things about me." Ron's fist thumped down on the desk, making the mic jump. "I changed the code to make a point to you, woman, and you—"

"That's enough." Vanessa's voice was loud enough to startle both of them into silence. She kept it at a professional level, but this was her take-no-shit tone, the one she pulled out on her most stubborn patients. They both turned to stare at her.

"We are here to discuss how to handle conflict in a healthy way. I asked you to keep it respectful, and you raised your voice and hit my desk."

Ron's mouth snapped shut.

Vanessa plowed on, the words falling out of her. "I've seen a lot of broken relationships. And this is the way it starts. Bad communication. Name calling. Willfully misunderstanding one another, and not really listening. I don't think that's what you came here for. Is it?"

"No. It's not." Emily shot her an apologetic look. Ron seemed stunned into silence.

"It's my job to help people communicate better," she went on. "I have a lot of experience with that, and I'm good at it. But I have to be honest, it's hard for me when clients get angry and aggressive in my office. I'll tell you why, since you asked for more of my experiences."

She sucked in a breath. "My parents' marriage was awful. I won't tell you all the details, but I have some lasting trauma from it. Hearing verbal abuse was a daily part of my life growing up. So I went to college to learn how to fix other people's marriages. That should have been my first sign I'm a hopeless romantic. I try to save relationships that seem doomed. And I've been successful at it so far. Except in my own life."

She let out a hiccupy little laugh. Ron and Emily stared at her, silent.

"In my own life, I've bailed out of relationships at the first sign of trouble. I realized that about myself recently. I end things at the first hint of conflict, because I can't stand the thought of becoming like my parents. Some of my exes have been genuine red flags. Like the one with the credit card thing. But some of them probably didn't deserve it. Some were nice guys who I tossed out because I didn't trust them. My last boyfriend ghosted me, and I assumed he was cheating, even when he wasn't. Because that's my default. A lack of trust. And that's what you two are dealing with as well."

She focused her gaze on Emily. "You're going to have to let go of monitoring all his thoughts and behaviors. It's making you miserable."

"And you." She swung around to Ron, keeping her voice professional, but firm. "Make an effort to listen to what she needs. She needs reassurance, not you brushing off all her concerns with a laugh. And don't call her 'woman' or 'young lady' anymore. She's right, women really don't like that shit."

She stopped her speech, chest heaving. The room was silent. Emily's mouth hung open.

With a shaking hand, Vanessa reached for the record button on the laptop and hit pause. She cleared her throat.

"Well. That got off topic. Again. I'm sorry if I—"

"No, no," Emily said, her voice high and too polite. "I think … I think it was good for us to hear that. Don't you, Ron?"

"I … uh," he stammered. She'd never seen him at a loss for a comeback.

"We'll get going now." Emily put a hand on her husband's arm, and for once, he stayed and waited for her, rather than leaving the office ahead of her. "But maybe you have enough material from us for your podcast now?"

An uncertain smile formed at the corner of Emily's mouth. "It was definitely ... more juicy than last time?"

Vanessa resisted the urge to slam her forehead down on the desk. "Of course. We can be done for today."

She gave them a weak wave and watched them leave the office. Then she did drop her head onto the desk. She was incapable of recording a decent podcast. She wouldn't ask Ron and Emily back for a third time, and she should delete this recording right now and throw in the towel.

She'd put herself out there for this episode, gotten far more personal than she'd intended, and look where it had landed her. Too exposed, her problems clearly so much worse than those of her clients.

She'd failed Ron and Emily, too. The podcast had stirred up old resentments for them, rather than making their relationship better. The entire purpose of the podcast was to help people, and she hadn't exactly done that.

She shut down her recording software and dragged the recording file into the trash folder of her laptop. Where it belonged.

Noah's apartment key was in her purse, and he'd said she could use it anytime. She could go there tonight after work and be enfolded in one of his comforting bear hugs. It wouldn't fix this terrible day, but it might make her feel better.

Not all her relationships had failed. She had something with him, something that was feeling more and more like the real thing. If she had Noah to come home to, everything in her life would make sense, because all her failures had been leading up to finding him. She could go to him when she needed comfort, and he'd be there to catch her.

Chapter 16

Noah arrived home earlier than usual with a bag of groceries balanced on one arm. Vanessa had texted that she was working late tonight, so instead of going to her place, he'd picked up ingredients for dinner and headed home. He was whistling as he unlocked the front door, but the sound died in his teeth when he saw the small stack of cardboard boxes and single suitcase by the front door.

His stomach dropped. "Silvia?"

"I'm here." She stuck her head out the kitchen door.

"What's going on?" he asked.

He set the bag of groceries on the couch before he dropped it. Because it looked like …

"I'm moving out," she said with a big smile. "I found a place this afternoon. It's on the west side of town, really nice, with a bay window and a big kitchen. I can move in right away, they said."

"How …" He sank down onto the couch, pulse racing. "I thought …"

After her conversation with Vanessa, the logical next step was for her to do counseling for a while. Not move out.

She made her way down the hall toward him, the boot still slowing her progress. When she got to the living room, she stopped in front of him, hands on her hips.

"How did I find a place? I took the bus. Or do you mean how did I pack all my stuff by myself? I can lift things just fine, you know." A hint of her sharp temper colored the words.

"I know you can." His head spun. "I just meant … I didn't know you'd decided to do this."

"I had a phone appointment with a counselor yesterday evening. While you were gone." She raised an eyebrow at him, but didn't comment further on his absence.

"Oh."

"It was only a start, but after talking to her, I knew. I made a decision yesterday, but I've been telling you what I wanted all along. You don't need me here anyway. Not even to cook dinner."

"But … how did you pay the deposit?"

She folded her arms across her chest. "I do have some money of my own, you know. My mother always told me, keep part of your money separate, and when I left home, I had a small savings."

"I didn't know."

"Now you do."

He sank heavily onto the couch, fighting the nausea churning his gut. "You're really not going back to Dad."

"I can't." Her voice softened, and she sank onto the couch next to him, patted his forearm. "I know that's what you wanted to happen. But I know for sure now that I need space to be on my own. To figure out what I want, what I like."

He drew in a deep breath. "I want you to have that. I can see how you need it, honestly. I just …"

"I know this is hard for you. And I know you would let me stay here," she said, her tone gentle. "Maybe you even think you want that. But it's not what you want."

He swallowed. "Who's going to help you out at home? If you have trouble."

Her mouth turned up in a smile. "Well, I know I won't be rid of you. And some of the women at temple volunteered to come help me out with chores, if I need it."

"That's nice of them."

"I know you want to protect me. Keep me safe. You think like your dad in that way. You want to make sure I go to all my appointments, take all my meds. But I can do those things alone."

"I know you can. Of course you can." He pressed his lips together.

Dad had assumed she couldn't take care of herself. And that was part of the reason she'd had to leave.

"I don't want to be like Dad," he said after a beat. "At least not in that way."

"Then let me go. Help me start my new life."

His eyes burned, and he pinched the bridge of his nose. "Okay. Of course I'll help you. You know I'll do that."

"Noah. Look at me."

He raised his eyes to meet hers, and they brimmed with warmth. And excitement. She was thrilled about the change, and he had to try to share her happiness. Even if it meant his parents staying apart.

"I'll always be here for you," she said. "That's not going to change."

"I know. But I wish you and Dad could have talked at least—"

A key jingling in the front door lock brought both their heads around.

Vanessa couldn't have picked today of all days to come here, but she had. A moment later, her auburn cloud of hair appeared in the doorway.

"Noah? I hope you don't mind, I—" She stopped dead when she saw him sitting with Silvia on the couch. Her voice had been uncertain to start with, and now it died away to nothing.

Silvia straightened next to him. Her brows went up.

"She has your key," she said.

He froze. "I'll explain."

"Noah lent me his key the other day," Vanessa said in a rush, lying to cover for him. "I was stopping by to return it, but I'll go now. Let me just get out of your way."

It was wrong, all wrong, for her to try to save his ass now from the colossal mistake he'd made by hiding her in the first place.

She was halfway out the door already when Noah stood.

"No. Vanessa, stop."

He went to her, guided her inside, and shut the door behind her. He put his arm around her waist and drew her close as Silvia watched them, comprehension dawning on her face.

Vanessa was silent, as if trying to disappear, and that was not okay. She deserved to be here. And maybe this was the worst possible time to break the news to Silvia, but she'd just dropped some big news of her own.

"Vanessa and I are dating," he told her, though she'd clearly guessed that. "We were dating last year, then we took a break. But we're back together now. That's why she has my key."

"And why didn't you feel you could tell me this?" Silvia

rose from the couch, vibrating with tension. Against his side, Vanessa's body was stiff and still.

"No, don't answer that." Silvia made a slashing gesture in the air. "I already know why. You wanted to protect me. To let me think my being here wasn't interrupting your life."

"You know I wanted you here. I wanted to give you space to figure things out, before I brought my personal stuff into it."

She narrowed her eyes at him. "You wanted to give me space because you thought I was fragile. Well, I am not. Did you think I couldn't handle knowing about your life?"

"No, I—"

"And when did you break up? When I got here?"

His stomach dropped further, because Silvia always figured these things out. She knew him too well.

"Yeah." He blew out a breath. "It was after you moved in. I didn't mean for it to go like that, but that's what happened."

"Unbelievable." Silvia shook her head.

She turned to Vanessa. "I'm sorry you're hearing this argument. I like you, and I think you and Noah are a very good match. But my son doesn't share very much of himself. I'm sorry my being here made problems for your relationship."

"Oh, no, it didn't—" Vanessa spoke for the first time since coming in the door.

"I'll leave you two to talk," Silvia interrupted. "I'm sure he'll tell you I'm moving out tomorrow. Maybe it will give you two some space. Which he could have had at any time, if he'd talked to me."

She shot another sharp gaze his way before heading down the hall. Her bedroom door shut with a soft click. As soon as she was out of earshot, Vanessa wrenched herself away from his side, her hand going to the doorknob.

"I should go now." Her voice sounded calm, almost pleasant, but it was her client voice, the one she put on in tense situations. Her hand shook on the knob, and she fumbled her first two attempts to get the door open.

"Vanessa, wait. Can we talk? Baby, what are you doing?"

Her shoulders had started to shake, too, and this was bad. She was trying to get away from him as fast as possible, and he had to stop her, talk to her before she did.

"What's going on?"

"I think I just made a huge mistake." Her voice wobbled. "I shouldn't have come here. But I had a bad day at work, and I thought … You said it would be okay if I came over." The last part sounded torn out of her.

He put a hand on her shoulder, bewildered at her reaction.

"It is okay for you to come over. Silvia and I … We were having a hard conversation when you walked in. But she's okay."

"This wasn't how we were supposed to tell her. She's mad at you now, and that's my fault."

Understanding dawned. Vanessa hated conflicts because of seeing her parents fight growing up. She was freaked out because she thought she'd caused a family fight.

"Silvia has a temper, and she gets mad at me sometimes, but she likes you. You heard her say so. I'm sorry she had to find out about us all of a sudden, though."

Her shoulders rose on a shaky little inhale. "Did you want her to find out?"

"Yes. I was ready for us not to be a secret anymore. Weren't you?"

"I thought I was. But I didn't want it to happen like that. And you couldn't actually tell her until I walked in on you."

His stomach flip-flopped. "But I did tell her. I didn't try to hide anything today."

"You told her because you had to." She shook her head, looking dazed. "That's your pattern, isn't it? You don't volunteer things, and you don't speak up for yourself and what you want. You wanted to be an engineer, and you didn't. You wanted to be with me, too, but you couldn't ever say it to her, not in the whole last year."

"I—" He swallowed, because she was right about that part.

"And now she's moving out." Her voice held a thread of tension. "Right after she talked to me about counseling."

"Not because of you," he said quickly. "She'd been talking about moving out for months. After you talked to her, she spoke to a counselor, and then she decided to rent her own place. Like you told her, she might not be ready to try again with him."

Her face froze. He'd said the wrong thing, in the exact wrong way.

"I have to go," she said. "I made a mistake coming here. I already said that. Oh, my God."

He reached for her arm, but she flinched away.

"It's not your fault," he told her, his heart a desperate drumbeat in his chest.

"I shouldn't have involved myself at all with your parents. I made a mistake. Because now you're always going to associate me with their breaking up."

"I don't—"

"And I'm happy for Silvia. I really am. It sounds like she needs this change. But I shouldn't have been the one to help her make it. I should have waited until you figured out the situation yourself. That was why you ghosted me in the first place. I should have steered clear of getting involved with you. That would have been smarter. But I'm not very smart about love." Her mouth turned down, her eyes shining with tears.

His stomach clenched, because she'd said love. She'd never said she loved him, not once. Not when they were dating before, and not since.

He reached for her again, the movement automatic, but she slid under his arm and wrenched the door open.

"I have to go, Noah."

"I don't understand … Wait. Are you breaking up with me?"

"I think I have to. I can't do this. I can't be in the middle of this."

She slipped through the crack in the door and bolted down the stairs from his apartment before he could get out another word. His brain had stopped, frozen still, and he stood gripping the door frame. Stuck in more ways than one.

She'd left him, like he'd left her ten months ago, and a hole had been ripped in the center of his chest. If this was what she'd felt like back then, he deserved every bit of this pain.

By tomorrow afternoon, Silvia would be gone, too. He'd lost both of them in less than an hour.

He hadn't learned anything about communication in the last month. He'd broken up with Vanessa last year because he'd refused to tell her what was going on in his personal life, and now Silvia wasn't speaking to him for the same reason.

He doesn't share very much of himself, she'd said.

Vanessa had let him in, let him start to see what she needed to be happy. She had to be able to count on him. He'd invited her to come to him when she needed him, and he'd let her leave here thinking she never should have involved herself with his family mess.

Chapter 16

He'd thought he could handle his parents' breakup and re-starting his own relationship at the same time, but he'd mixed the two together in a dangerous way. He never should have kept her a secret.

And now they were over again. He rubbed a hand over his chest, where the pain was a physical presence setting up shop, his heart missing a vital cog.

On autopilot, he made his way to the kitchen. Silvia would need dinner before her big moving day tomorrow. They'd need to go to the store for some housewares, then he'd swing by Dad's house to load any furniture she wanted into the truck.

They were the last few things she'd let him do for her. And then he'd have to figure out what to do with himself alone.

Chapter 17

Vanessa got herself into her apartment, shut the door behind her, and leaned against it heavily. She dropped her bag on the floor and sucked in deep breaths, continuing the process of coming down from the adrenaline rush of running away from Noah.

She'd sprinted to her car as if a monster was chasing her, and it was partly true, but the monster was her own shortcomings and failures.

And maybe flat-out running had been a tiny bit of an overreaction, but the sheer panic, complete with racing heart and full-body sweat—that had been real. The moment Silvia cast her first sharp remark in Noah's direction, all her calm had fled, and old instincts had kicked in, telling her to get out of there before the fight got worse.

She peeled off her coat, tossed it onto the couch, and went to the kitchen, where she drained a glass of water and stood staring into the sink. No way could she handle dinner tonight.

She'd gone to Noah's apartment because he'd told her he

wanted her there. And of course, the very first time she used his key, it blew up in her face. She'd shattered Noah's secret, not that she'd liked being his secret in the first place.

And Silvia was moving out, and even though it wasn't her fault, she'd put her two cents in there, so she'd been involved in the decision.

It had to be some kind of world record, breaking up two marriages in one day. A hysterical laugh wanted to bubble out of her. She'd left the mess of Ron and Emily's marriage at her office and walked straight into another disaster.

A memory of her last conversation with her parents flashed into her mind. Their barely suppressed anger when she'd suggested they needed help. Her pulse racing, everything in her body telling her to hide before the yelling started. But she'd stayed put, used all her grad school therapy training, so sure she could make a difference.

It hadn't changed her parents' relationship. They'd kicked her out instead.

All her counseling training hadn't saved Silvia's marriage, either, or Emily's. Or her own relationship, for that matter.

She kicked off her shoes with vicious force.

"Red flags. I specialize in red flags."

She'd seen this one coming a mile away. The man had kept her a secret from his mother. His mother, who lived with him, and who he didn't want to move out. She'd known it was a bad idea, and she'd still taken a chance. Because she always kept trying, even when she always failed at love. A hundred percent of the time.

An hour and a hot bath later, she curled under her lace-covered duvet, making herself into the smallest ball possible. She pulled the heavy comforter over her head and took calming breaths.

Every bad experience has a lesson to teach.

Learn from failures and get back up again.

Positive self-talk really did not help when it was the second worst night of your life.

She hugged herself tight and tried not to think of Noah's face, frozen with shock and sadness as she'd run away from him.

Maybe she'd overreacted. But maybe he also needed to get his life together.

What they'd had for the last two weeks had felt real. It might have been the foundation of something, if not for the fact that the whole thing had been built on a giant lie to his family.

Tomorrow, she'd sift through this mess, pick herself up, and figure out what went wrong. But for tonight, she was a turtle in its shell, a cringing snail, and she was not coming out.

* * *

Three days later, she had a complete podcast episode, almost ready to post. Just a couple of short segments left to record, and she would publish it. It wasn't how she'd planned for the show to launch, but sometimes you had to lean into your worst mistakes. It was amazing how far denial, extra caffeine, and a few good wardrobe choices could take you.

She'd woken up the morning after her breakup, dressed for work in her screaming red vegan leather skinny pants, matching vest, white dress shirt, and three-inch pumps, and gone to work determined to interview every one of her coworkers about their worst fights and breakups. Surely, other people had stories as bad as hers to tell, and maybe those stories of conflict held lessons for her listeners. And for her.

Most of them were happy to share. Sophie told the story of how she'd organized her college boyfriend's closet by color gradations, and he'd walked in and yelled at her when he saw it. It wasn't her fault she had OCD, and the man could have chosen to see her organization skills as a strength, but he hadn't.

Maria, the family counselor on staff, described fighting with her ex on a three-day road trip, in which they'd pause the argument to fall asleep at night, wake up each morning, and re-start the fight.

As Vanessa laughed along with the older woman at the memory, her own memories from the other night at Noah's threatened to consume her, and she fought them back. She wouldn't think about him, because if she dwelled on everything she'd done wrong, she'd never finish this project. Getting the podcast going was the priority now.

At least she'd proven that everyone had a story to tell, and some even rivaled her own collection of disasters.

This afternoon, she sat across her desk from Cameron, who'd agreed to record for a few minutes with her because she'd seen him leaving the clinic after 9:00 p.m. on the surveillance camera. Again.

When she'd confronted him about it, he'd been cagey, unwilling to share this time why he'd been there so late. So she'd used his guilt to leverage him into recording this episode, in exchange for more promises she wouldn't tell Ben about how much he'd been here this week.

He folded his forearms on her desk and glared at her mic.

"All right. Let's get this over with."

"Don't sound so excited about it," she teased him.

"You blackmailed me into this. In the most friendly way," he added.

"Quit staying here so late, and then I won't have any material to blackmail you with."

He shifted around on his chair, cutting his gaze away from her. "It won't happen again. I promise."

Interesting. Cameron never apologized for his back-breaking hours. Something else was going on. Still, she wouldn't pry into that right now, because today, she had the joy of prying into his love life instead.

"Okay. We're recording now," she announced after hitting the button. "So Cameron, we've been sharing all our worst or most interesting arguments, and what happened because of them. I believe that through arguing, we can sometimes do some of our best communicating. So if you wouldn't mind, tell our listeners about the worst fight you've had with a partner, past or present."

"This is going to make me sound like a nerd, just to warn you," he said.

"Listeners, Cameron is a huge nerd," she told the microphone. "You can't see him right now. But today he's wearing suspenders with ... What language is that printed on them?"

"Klingon." He cleared his throat. "Not that anyone cares."

"They're very nice suspenders."

"Thank you."

"Okay, so your argument story is as nerdy as your office attire, according to you. Go on."

"So, I had a girlfriend in college. We went to sci-fi cons a lot, and one time, in the car on the way there, we got into an argument about which episodes her favorite character appeared in."

"Sounds serious."

"It felt that way at the time. Anyway, I wouldn't let her search for the answers online. She was cosplaying that day, and she'd let me put her phone in my pocket."

"Ouch. Withholding the internet."

He rolled his eyes. "Anyway. I had all the episodes memorized—"

"As you do."

"—And when we pulled into the parking lot, I handed her the phone. She looked it up and found out I was right. Then she didn't speak to me the rest of the day. Kind of ruined the whole thing."

"That's it? That's the worst fight you've ever been in?" she asked, incredulous.

"I told you it wasn't interesting."

Vanessa leaned forward. "No, I am interested. Haven't you ever lost your temper and yelled? At least let out a badly timed insult?"

Cameron's brows dropped. "It doesn't make any sense to do that. Why would I want to lose my temper at someone?"

The man was devoid of emotions. She'd wondered on occasion if he was an android.

"Well." She cleared her throat. "This is a good example of how everyone's emotional landscape is different. And how one couple's mild argument can be another couple's biggest fight. Thank you for sharing, by the way."

"No problem," he grumbled.

She punched the pause button on the recording, and Cameron got out of there as fast as he could. There was one segment left to record, edit into the show, and then she'd publish the episode.

She shut her office door for privacy, settled herself back at her desk, and hit record again.

"I've had a few days to go over all the material I've recorded, and I wanted to come back and recap some of what you heard. I want to restate that I started this podcast with the intention of helping people work through their relationship issues. When the first couple of recording attempts ended with people fighting, I thought I'd failed. But then I reminded myself of something I already know: that failure is part of the process. Fights are part of the process of a relationship."

"With R and E's written permission, I'm leaving in their argument. I've also left in the parts of this recording where I talked about my own experiences with my parents' marriage. That was not something I intended to talk about, but I think it's important for people to hear for a couple of reasons. If you are a parent, please be aware of how your relationship might be affecting your children, and get help if you need it. But I also left in that part so you can see I'm only human. I know how to help others communicate better, but I have my own set of experiences that act as a filter for all my relationships."

She drew in a deep breath.

"I've been afraid of failure, afraid of fighting. I label everything a red flag or a disaster, when sometimes it's not. I don't think I always knew that about myself, but I learned it over time, in part through creating this podcast, and in part through my relationships."

"If you're listening to this, wondering how your relationship got into bad shape and how it can be fixed, please know that you're not alone. Maybe through community, and through hearing the experiences of others, we can all be inspired to keep trying. Next week, we're going to give some more real-life examples of strategies you can use in moments of tension, to avoid some of these fights altogether. I've got some great new interviews planned, so please join us again. And thank you for listening."

She hit the stop button and didn't listen to the replay. If she did, she might lose her nerve. Instead, she added the segment and Cameron's interview to her show using the editing software, and hit upload before she could have second thoughts.

It would go live on all the podcast platforms in twenty-four hours, and until then, she could no longer edit it.

"Episode one is a wrap," she told her empty office.

She shut her laptop and rubbed a hand over her forehead. Of all the messed up things she'd done in her relationships, never had she posted a verbal account of them for thousands of people to listen to. This could go over badly. Or possibly very well.

That afternoon, she packed up her bag to go home on time. No more staying late and starving herself, worrying about the podcast. It would either succeed or fail.

Her office phone rang right as she was heading out the door. She almost ignored it, but went to pick up the call.

"Vanessa speaking."

"Vanessa? It's Emily. I'm so glad I caught you in person."

She set her bag down. "Emily? Is everything going okay?"

"Fine, fine." The other woman gave a nervous laugh. "I just wanted to thank you for the other day."

"You wanted to thank me? I felt like I should apologize to you."

"No, no. Completely unnecessary. I was calling to tell you

that Ron and I ... Well, we'd decided to separate the day before we came to that recording session. I went into the session not feeling sure about it. And afterward ... I knew it was the right choice, at least for now. I don't know what will happen in the long run, but that conversation helped me get the clarity I needed. So thank you. What you said changed things for us."

Vanessa sank into her chair. "It did?"

"Yes. But in a good way. It's like you broke the ice on all the things we weren't talking about. Ron is acting different. I didn't think it was possible to shake him up, but you did it. He's talking to me in a different way than he used to. He listens when I ask him questions. I don't know how to describe it. But thank you."

"Thank you for telling me. You have no idea how much ... Sometimes it's nice to hear I helped."

"You really did. And you were the one who taught me I should express appreciation out loud. I also want to say, I hope things get better for you, too. You deserve it, Vanessa."

Unexpected tears burned her eyes. "Thank you. That means a lot."

She set the phone down and stared at it for a few minutes.

Emily had sounded so happy, so relieved. She'd found freedom in taking a few steps away from her relationship, like Silvia had. Not every relationship could or should be saved.

People found their courage in different ways through relationships. For some, it took bravery to end a relationship. For other people, the courage was in beginning a relationship at all. Or trying again, facing their problems head-on.

She'd been brave every time she let herself start a relationship. But she hadn't been particularly brave three days ago. She'd run away from Noah, and broken her own heart in the process.

She let the thought fully form, for the first time in days. She was heartbroken. Noah was the other half of her heart. When she pictured a green flag, he was the only man who came to mind. For all her issues, she'd let herself go with him, let herself trust him for real.

She had changed in the last few weeks. Being with him had changed her, and she wasn't the same, even though her knee-jerk reaction had ruined everything.

He hadn't called or texted her since the night she'd left, and he never would. He had his own problems to deal with, and had all along. And texting wasn't his strong suit. After the way she'd acted, he probably thought he was better off letting her go for real this time.

And if her stupid, foolish heart still missed him, she'd have to deal with it and move on. Because they'd had their second chance, but third chances were too much to hope for.

Chapter 18

Noah pulled hard on the orange nylon strap securing the last vending machine to the trailer bed. He'd tightened it too far, and it'd be a pain to unload later. Like Jessie had predicted, the oldest machine had been a beast to fix, taking much longer than his original estimate of three days. After replacing all the coils and rewiring the electrical, the thing was fully functional.

Which was more than he could say for himself. He'd barely eaten or slept in the last week, his stomach a constant sour churn. Home was too quiet. Work was long and frustrating, with nothing to look forward to at the end of the day.

These last few years had been all about making the business survive. But Vanessa had reminded him he'd wanted to be doing something different with his life at one point. He'd let family obligations drag him in another direction, trying to be the good son out of some misguided belief that if he did everything other people wanted, then nothing would have to change.

But Silvia had left Dad, and Vanessa had left him, and he wasn't any happier for his sacrifices. Vanessa must be relieved to be free of him, though.

He rubbed a hand over the center of his chest. Heartburn had been his constant companion this week.

After she'd walked out on him and Silvia moved out the next morning, his first impulse had been to go home and hide in his apartment, watch TV, and not come out for a week. But he couldn't hide under the table from this one, so he'd come to work the next day, and the next.

He could go on like this forever, one day after the other, until he retired—probably alone like Dad. Or he could make some changes. They wouldn't get Vanessa to come back, but they'd give him a sense of purpose. He'd never done well alone, especially with being left behind. Now he'd have more interesting work as a companion at least.

A week after he and Vanessa broke up, he and Jessie sat down for an informal staff meeting, and he outlined some changes he'd planned for the shop. Jessie was beyond thrilled with the new direction for the business, and a sliver of relief broke through his general bleak mood.

He jumped off the truck bed in time to see Dad's car pull into the parking lot. He'd asked the old man to come by this afternoon, and Aaron was nothing if not punctual after so many years working at the shop.

"Noah." Dad pulled him into a one-armed hug and slapped him on the back. "Good to see you."

Aaron laid a hand on the metal side of the vending machine. "I see you got the old girls up and running again."

"They're not girls. But yeah."

"Right." Dad shifted his gaze to the side, looking almost

uncomfortable. "It's good you texted me. I was planning to stop by today anyway. I have something important to tell you."

Noah's stomach dropped, and he put a hand there reflexively. Dad and Silvia were getting divorced. With nothing tying her here, Silvia might move back to Mexico, and he'd never see her again. It was one thing for them to separate, but this would be much worse.

He sank down into a crouch on the low metal edge of the trailer. "I don't … I'm not sure I want to know."

"Son, what's wrong? You just turned whiter than a sheet." Aaron sat down next to him, resting a hand on his back. "Are you sick?"

"You're getting divorced. That's what you came here to tell me." He couldn't look at Dad right now. The eye contact would be too much.

"No. God, no. That's what you thought? Listen to me. It's not that, okay?"

"It's not?"

"It's nothing bad, I promise. Actually, I think it's pretty good news." He sounded almost shy.

Noah's head jerked up to look at him now. Dad was honest-to-God blushing.

"Silvia texted me the other day," he said, looking more than pleased with himself.

"She didn't."

"She did. The day she moved out from your place. She texted me. For the first time in almost a year. I know, I couldn't believe it, either."

"Why did she … What did she say?"

"She said she wanted me to know she was starting over on her own, but that she would be open to talking to me. Son, I raced over to her place twenty minutes later. Told her I'd help her unpack. Thought that would be a good excuse, but she said no, she didn't want my help."

Noah snorted a laugh. "She wouldn't."

"No. So I watched her unpack. I sat there on her couch, which, thank you for getting the furniture moved in."

"Not a problem." He shook his head, dazed, while Dad continued.

"I watched her unpack, and finally she sat down next to me and just looked at me. Didn't offer me a drink or anything. You know how intense she can look at you."

"I do."

"And I felt ... God, Noah, I hadn't even seen her in almost a year. I started crying, I was so happy to see her face."

"Dad. That's ..."

He was at a loss for words. He'd never seen Dad cry. Ever. Much less admit to it.

"I know. I just kept saying I was sorry. I couldn't think of anything else to say."

"You should learn to communicate better."

Dad shook his head. "Don't I know it. Then afterward, I was a complete mess, and she gave me a box of tissues and told me she still had feelings for me. She said ... You're not gonna believe this."

"What?"

"She said she still loves me, but she doesn't want to live with me. She said she wants to try to reconcile, but we can't live in the same place while we do that. Or maybe ever."

Noah held his breath. For a traditionalist like Dad, that would have been a deal breaker in the past.

"What'd you tell her?" he asked.

"I told her yes, of course," Aaron said, incredulous. "I'd do anything to spend one day with her again."

A smile threatened to take over Noah's face. "Yeah?"

"Heck yeah. Let me tell you, retirement taught me a few things. One, with so much time on my hands, I realized all the things we never talked about. I can see why she didn't want to be stuck in the house with me there all the time. Then after she was gone, I realized how quiet it was. How empty."

"I can see that." Noah knew exactly how lonely an empty apartment felt. "So you're really … getting back together?"

"We're going to try. But keep living apart."

"I can see that working out. She needs her own space. She needs to figure out who she is apart from you."

Dad's eyes widened. "That's what she said. But she also said love is the reason why we're here on earth. And she didn't want to give up on it."

Noah froze at hearing Vanessa's words repeated back, then forced himself to relax his posture. She would be glad to know her conversation with Silvia had made a difference.

"That's really great, Dad. You have no idea how much I hoped this would happen."

The old man's expression softened. "I think I do have an idea. I'm sorry you got caught in the middle of this."

"I didn't mind."

"I know you didn't. You're a good son."

Noah drew in a deep inhale. "You might disagree with me in a minute. When I tell you why I asked you to come out today."

Dad's eyes sharpened. "Okay. What is it?"

"I sold half the business. To Jessie. I made her the manager, and I'm hiring an assistant manager to help her."

He got ready for an earful. But Dad leaned back, bracing his hands behind him on the trailer.

"Huh," was all he said.

"You're not mad?"

His expression turned thoughtful. "Not mad, no. I guess this isn't really what you wanted."

"It's not. I'm applying for engineering contract work. It'll be part time, and I'll still help out around here part time. But Jessie's in charge now."

The old man's brow lowered. "I think … She'll do a great job," he said slowly.

"No one better. She's got all the same skills you or I have. And she was thrilled at the raise. And the shop's name change."

"Name change?" Now Dad sounded alarmed.

"Yep. The shop's gonna be Green and Blue Appliance Repair. On account of her blue hair."

A laugh burst out of the older man. "I like that. I do." He slapped Noah on the back. "Didn't think this is what would be happening in my life two years after retirement. But I can honestly say I'm not mad about it. As long as I have Silvia."

"You two were made for each other. If you couldn't make it work together …" He swallowed. "I don't know that I'd believe anyone could. But listen to her. Talk to her about what she wants to talk about."

"I will, son. And you keep talking to us, too. I'm glad you told me you were ready for a change. Not sure why I didn't see it a long time ago."

He hadn't seen it a long time ago because he'd never paid close attention to his family's inner workings. But there was no need to say so. Maybe everything was about to change, and it was enough for now that Dad had listened to Silvia. That was the most important thing.

They stood and Dad made a show of brushing the dust off his pants, clearly trying to return to normal after the emotional conversation. There were only so many feelings the old man could take before he had to turn them off again.

He watched Dad drive away, heading back to Silvia. They were having dinner together, he'd said, looking as delighted as if they were going on a hot first date. And maybe they were, in a way. The first date of their new life together. The one where they listened and made space for one another, and did all those good communication things Vanessa talked about.

He wouldn't get to go home to Vanessa tonight. But some pieces of his life had been re-knitted together.

For a few weeks, getting to have her had seemed within reach. But as she'd pointed out, he'd poured himself into saving Silvia and Dad's relationship, as well as Dad's business, and left too little for himself.

At home, he cooked a frozen dinner for one and thought about Silvia cooking dinner in her new apartment. She was no doubt making something better than this. Maybe one of Dad's favorites to welcome him to their new life. Together, but standing on their own.

He was happy for them, he really was. He took a few bites standing at the sink, then left the half-full plate on the counter to go sit on the couch.

It was a bad sign when he went off his food. He hadn't lost his appetite like this since … well, since he was nine, and decided to live off crackers and water under the dining room table.

The apartment was too silent, so he flipped on the TV. But the cheerful sitcoms with their happy laugh tracks grated on his ears, and the action movies were too jarring. He shut the TV off again.

His phone offered more distractions. But social media apps were full of happy pictures of college friends with their wives and kids, on vacation or celebrating someone's birthday.

This was ridiculous. He'd been alone for less than two weeks, and he couldn't handle the silence. He opened his podcast app, intending to listen to an auto repair podcast he caught every week, when a new notification popped up.

The Well Relationship, episode one, was available to download. He'd bookmarked the show page back when Vanessa told him her plans for the podcast.

In slow motion, his finger went to the play button. He had to hear her voice, but it was also going to kill him. He wanted to know what she'd say, but he didn't want to know. He was helpless to resist her, like always.

He set the phone on the couch next to him, shut his eyes, and let himself soak in the sound of her voice for the first few minutes. He pictured her face with perfect clarity—the intelligent green eyes with their hints of sadness lurking behind her cat-eye glasses. His body remembered the feel of her, down to the brush of her hand against his and her weight in his arms. His chest ached in a way that never eased unless she was nearby.

The episode started off cheerful and upbeat, but the conversation soon took a turn to more serious issues. When the guests' voices grew sharp and angry, he sat up straighter on the couch and picked up the phone, as if he could stop the people inside it from fighting.

Vanessa didn't do well with the angry kind of fights. But she was a professional. She could handle one arguing couple.

He listened to her wrangle the couple into silence, and then he listened to her speak her own truth, putting it out there for the whole world. Because his woman was vulnerable like that.

Fragile and strong at the same time.

"In my own life, I bail out of relationships at the first sign of trouble. I realized that recently," she said. "My last boyfriend ghosted me, and I assumed he was cheating, even when he wasn't. Because that's my default. A lack of trust."

His hand froze on the phone, because something clicked into place he hadn't seen before. She'd been scared of going deeper into their relationship. Ten months ago, she'd been the one to suggest they break up first, even though he'd agreed far too quickly.

She'd rarely let him come to her house, a year ago. She'd never let him be in control of their plans. Because she hadn't trusted him, hadn't been able to let go.

But she'd done those things during the last month. She'd let him in, in ways he was now a hundred percent sure she'd never let anyone else in before.

He hadn't called her or texted her in a week because he'd been so sure she never wanted to see him again. But maybe she'd just been afraid. Afraid, and hurting.

He listened to the end of the show, squeezing his phone like it was a connection to her. When it ended, the podcast app switched to the next show in the queue, and he jabbed the button to turn it off.

He was going to have to go to her. She'd laid bare her entire self to the world, and he could do the same for her, one more time. If she told him to go, he'd leave her alone. But he'd never know unless he talked to her. Hiding out at home was not the answer.

He'd never been the best at communicating, but he'd gotten better. And for a short window of time, he'd figured out what she needed, and she'd let him give it to her. The purest sense of rightness he'd ever known had been taking care of her, and he wanted more of that feeling.

He knew what she needed, sure as he'd ever known anything. Vanessa Bernhard needed someone steady and reliable, someone who would always put her first. And he could be that man, if she'd still let him.

Chapter 19

Ben's return to the office after his honeymoon preceded him by a good ten minutes. Sophie walked past Vanessa's office door and rapped on the frame.

"Big man's back. His car just pulled in." She sounded a little out of breath.

"Thanks for the heads up." Vanessa shook her head and bent over her laptop again, smiling to herself.

People got so flustered by Ben, when there was no reason to be intimidated. Just because he was six foot three, never smiled, and dressed like he was heading to a funeral, didn't mean he was a scary guy. He'd turned out to be a lot softer than he seemed, especially since getting engaged. He was also one of her oldest friends.

He stuck his head in her office door a few minutes later. "Still holding down the fort for me, I see."

She jumped up from her desk to give him a quick hug. "It's so good to see you. You look tan."

His olive skin was several shades deeper than when he'd left two weeks ago. He wore his usual sharp three-piece suit, in charcoal gray today. He looked relaxed and happier than ever, though his smiles were still rare.

"Lots of sun on this trip," he said, leaning against the door frame.

"I've heard the Mediterranean is amazing this time of year. We got stuck with a bunch of snow here."

He nodded. "I heard. And more's coming tonight."

She groaned and rubbed a hand over her forehead. "Don't tell me that. I was supposed to get a new scraper for my car, and I forgot."

"Do you have a minute to catch up?" he asked. "I don't have any appointments until this afternoon."

"Of course."

Ben sat in one of her chairs, and she went back to her spot behind her desk. He studied her for a moment before speaking again.

"You look tired. Have you been working longer hours? I told you not to do that anymore."

After his own brush with debilitating anxiety, he worried about the mental health of his staff, one more reason he was a marshmallow on the inside. Well, maybe not exactly soft, but he cared.

"First of all, it's not nice to tell women they look tired. And second, I only worked late a few days, I promise," she reassured him. "I had a project I was getting off the ground, but I'm going home at the normal time these days."

"Good. And everyone else is, too?"

"I'm pretty sure." Which was a tiny lie, because Cameron had been here after hours at least three times last week. Probably more. Ben didn't check the security cameras very often, though.

"Good to hear. I want to know how our patient intake numbers are doing and get some appointment numbers from you, too. But first, your big news."

He planted his elbows on the armrests and leaned forward. "You didn't tell me you were starting a podcast. Why not?"

She drew in a deep inhale. She'd prepared for this conversation a hundred times in her mind.

"It was just an idea. Something I was playing around with. I wasn't even sure I could get it off the ground. I thought if I had a sample episode done by the time you came back, I could show you the value."

The corner of his mouth turned up, almost a smile. "You prefer to act first, and ask permission later. Not that you needed my permission."

"No, I know that. But I should have run it by you first. I guess I wanted to do something to help the clinic reach more people. Our staff are all booked for weeks, but I knew there had to be more ways we could reach out to the community. Your books were such a hit, I thought this could be another way to get the word out about us."

"My books reached one audience, but this will reach another." He leaned back in the chair again, steepling his fingers. "I listened to it on my way into work this morning."

"Oh God." For some reason, this scenario had not occurred to her. "Listen, I know there was some kind of personal stuff in there …"

"No, it was perfect. Really good. Personal, as you said, but also funny at times, and relatable. But Vanessa." He peered at her, his brown eyes full of concern. "That must have been a lot for you. Saying the things you did about your childhood, putting it out there for the whole world."

She shifted her gaze away from his. "It was a lot. These last two weeks have been … a lot. I'll tell you more about it later, but to make a long story short, I got back together with my ex, and then we broke up. Again."

He frowned. "I'm sorry to hear it."

"I'll be fine." *In a year or so. Or maybe never.*

She pasted on a bright smile, which he would know was fake, but she had to at least try. "At any rate, I'm glad you think the podcast went well. I've already got the next four episodes planned out."

"And the ratings?"

She flashed him a grin. "We debuted in the top ten shows in the health and wellness category."

"Of course we did. You did." He gave her an approving nod. "This will be great. You're right that this could take the clinic's reach to a new level."

"That's what we do, partner."

"Damn, we're good." He smiled at her, a genuine smile she'd bet most people in the clinic had never seen. "I'm glad to be back."

"It's good to have you back."

They caught up on the numbers, and a half hour later, Ben headed upstairs. He looked more relaxed than she'd ever seen him, his posture not as rigid and full of tension as it used to be. Maybe it was the two-week vacation, but she was pretty sure it was married life that had transformed him.

He was happy, for the first time since she'd known him. The difference love could make.

Not everyone got to have that, though. Some people were not successful in love, no matter how many times they tried.

She should make a podcast episode about it. She'd title it, "How to know when it's time to give up."

She'd never given up on love before. No matter how many times it beat her up, she kept coming back for more. Maybe it was time to reconsider her strategy.

Despite what she'd promised Ben, she did work late again that night. It was the first time she'd done it in a week, but she couldn't face going home yet. The apartment was too quiet, leaving her too much time alone with her thoughts. Better to be here, making progress on work.

The days were getting lighter now, edging closer to spring. The sky was bright gray, rather than pitch black, when she stepped out the front door of the clinic and confronted a wall of snow.

"Shit." She'd forgotten about the weather forecast, and she hadn't opened her curtains all afternoon. And now an early spring blizzard would ruin her commute home. She would have to make it out of the parking lot by herself this time.

Someone had shoveled the clinic's porch steps, even though the rest of the staff was long gone. Noah had always made sure things like that were taken care of. Her throat tightened, and she pulled her hood tightly over her head, ducked out into the storm, and headed to her car.

The snow was so thick, she didn't see him until she walked right into him. He stepped out in front of her, dark coat and bright blue beanie against the white snow. She'd have known who it was with her eyes closed.

She had a second to feel the scratchy canvas of his coat against her cheek before he put out his hands to steady her, holding her at arm's distance from him.

"You're here." They were the only words she could think of.

202

"I shoveled out your car. Scraped the windshield, too," he said.

"Thank you." Her heart accelerated, and she told it to calm down. Her heart wanted her to fling herself against him, but that was not what he'd come here for. He was just doing her a favor. He was a thoughtful person.

When he kept standing there, looking at her for a long minute, she broke the silence. "Well, like I said. Thank you. I should get going."

His hands clenched and unclenched by his sides, his chest puffing up and down. "I came to talk to you. But you're getting covered with snow, and I don't want you out in this."

This made more sense. He'd come to talk to her, maybe get some closure on how things had ended between them. But no way was she getting into the truck with him. Too close, too many memories.

"All right. Come on." She gestured for him to follow her back to the covered porch outside the clinic. It wasn't warm, but they wouldn't be snowed on while they talked, and they wouldn't be inside the close, intimate space of the clinic, either.

His footsteps crunched behind her in the snow. When she got onto the porch, she turned, squared her shoulders, and looked up at him. In the dim porch light, she saw his features clearly for the first time, and the aching feeling in her chest expanded.

He looked tired, same as her. His expression was determined, his jaw set. They did need to have some kind of conversation about this. Things had ended too abruptly, and now was as good a time as any to hash it out.

If only he didn't look so soft and warm and comforting. If he'd just pull her into a hug right now, maybe she could breathe for the first time in a week.

"So." She cleared her throat. "I guess I owe you an apology for how I ran out. That wasn't a good way to end things. It was immature of me, I know—"

"No." His voice was so firm, she stopped mid-sentence and stared at him.

"What do you mean, no?"

"I mean, no, you do not owe me an apology, and I don't need you to say you're sorry. I know why you did it."

"I … Okay. Why did I do it?"

"Because you got scared," he said. "That situation was your worst nightmare, and I realize that now. So if anyone needs to apologize, that would be me. I knew you had issues from your past, and I still stuck you in the middle of my parents' problems. I still asked you to keep our relationship a secret. Those were things I did, that I am sorry for."

"Can we agree we're both sorry for the parts we got wrong?" she asked.

"Okay." His breath puffed out of him in clouds, his expression so earnest that she couldn't break eye contact with him.

"I realized something else," he went on. "You were right about me. You said I don't speak up for myself and say what I want. But I knew inside that I wanted you all along. I just couldn't say it. Vanessa. When we were dating before, I put a down payment on a ring."

Her sharp inhale cut through the twilight.

"You what?"

"Right after Valentine's Day last year. I went to the store and put my first payment on it, and I could never bring myself to go get a refund, either. Even when we'd been broken up for months. I knew you were the one for me. I still know it." He tapped his fist against his chest.

"Noah …" She took a step toward him. He was either trying to get back together with her right now, or this added detail would heap more pain onto her worst breakup ever.

He was the world's most confusing man, and she loved him. So, so much.

He shook his head. "Let me just … Let me finish. I brought your mom's jewelry box back. I got it open, and before I tell you what's in it, I want you to know I got you another one."

"Okay. Why?" Had he broken the thing? One-word sentences seemed to be all she could manage, her heart lodged in her throat.

"Your mom's box didn't have anything in it."

"Oh." Of course it hadn't. All those years, she'd saved the box, hoping for some secret treasure that might connect her to her parents, but that was all a pipe dream. Silly imaginings from a rejected daughter.

"I got it open the night I brought it home," he went on. "Then it sat on my dresser for days, and I didn't know when or how I could give it back to you. I didn't want to disappoint you any more than you already had been. But then I listened to your podcast, and I knew what you needed."

He extracted two boxes from his coat pocket. "You need something real, a real promise from someone who's always going to be there for you, no matter what. And I'd already bought another box, anyway."

He handed both boxes to her. Her mother's heart-shaped box had been cracked open, and she slid it into her purse without a second glance. No need to look inside the thing she'd wondered about for more than a decade.

She hadn't seen the second box before. It was rectangular,

made of intricately carved cherry wood, comprising dozens of pieces fitted together.

"Is this from the antiques show?" she asked. "A puzzle box?"

"Yeah. I went back the next day after work and got it."

"And … what's inside of this one?"

He shoved his hands back into his pockets. "It's only yours when you're ready for it. If you never want it, it's fine. But it's the ring. Shit, I probably shouldn't have come out with it like that."

"You're giving me a ring. There's an engagement ring inside this box." She took another step closer to him, heart threatening to beat its way out of her chest.

"I know you don't want it yet. It's too soon. It doesn't even have to be an engagement ring. But I mean, that's why I bought it. And I'm giving it to you for safe keeping. I've got the instructions for how to open the box on a card in my wallet."

He rubbed a hand over the back of his neck. "I want you to know you already have it. You have my heart, and my commitment to you. It's yours when you need it, whether that's in a year, or never. It's there for you, always. Like I am."

"I know you are." She clutched the box in her fist with one hand and swiped tears from her cheeks with the back of her coat sleeve. "I felt you, even when you weren't around. Is that crazy of me?"

"No. I felt the same way."

"I trust you. More than anyone I've ever known. I promise you, I'm going to keep working on that. On letting myself trust you."

His eyes burned into her, and suddenly the short distance between them was too much.

"Will you please hug me now?" she asked. "I think … I really need a hug."

"Baby." He swept her into his arms, tight against him, and her body melted into his. She held the box against her chest between them. A shuddering inhale filled her lungs, then another. Relief, that's what this feeling was. Relief she'd found her person, after so many years of searching.

His hands wandered over her hair, stroked up and down her back, as if reassuring himself she was real.

He tilted her chin up to look at him, his eyes the deepest melting brown. "So does this mean you're back with me? I have you back?"

Her heart knew the answer. There was no hesitation left in her. The structure of her fears folded quietly, a house of cards coming down in the face of her certainty.

"Yes. You have me back."

"Good." His mouth came down on hers, and she let herself go, let herself be held in this perfect moment. He would always hold her up, and she'd do the same for him.

A minute later, he separated his mouth from hers.

"You're not driving home in this," he said.

"Okay." She rested her cheek on his chest, listening to his heart thump.

"I'll bring you back in the morning to get your car. But I want to take you home with me tonight."

"Yes. Take me home." She looped her elbow through his and let him hoist her into the still-warm truck cab. She buckled herself into the middle seat, so she could rest her head on his shoulder as he drove.

She let herself enjoy the ride, and the anticipation, because she'd never been one to give up on love. And she wouldn't start now.

Chapter 20

Six months later

Silvia set down her silver tea tray on the coffee table in front of them, and Noah reached for a scone. She'd piled the tray high with pottery mugs, plates of sweets, and a steaming teapot in the center.

She moved around faster and easier these days, without the boot. Her foot had healed completely, with no signs of lasting damage to the joint. He'd never seen her look happier or more at ease, in her new life with her own space.

"Thank you for making tea," he told her.

She waved a dismissive hand at him. "It was nothing. Now …" She sank into her armchair facing him and Vanessa. "Now, we make plans."

She'd invited them over to plan a surprise birthday party for Aaron, something the old man would never expect, and under normal circumstances, would probably hate. Noah's dad liked predictability and routines, not surprises. But he had a soft spot a mile wide for Silvia.

"Please, pour yourself a cup." Silvia gestured to the tray, and Vanessa reached for the teapot, pouring each of them a cup of bright red tea.

"Is this hibiscus?" she asked.

"Yes, with orange and honey. A light tea for the summer." Silvia blew on her cup before taking a sip. "So here is my idea. Noah, I'll need your help."

"I'm listening."

"We tell him the golf club called. Something came up with his membership, and he needs to go to the main office to clear it up."

"Oh, that'll get his attention," Noah said.

"I know." Silvia arched a brow. "Then, when he arrives, the clerk will tell him they're very sorry, the manager isn't available to speak with him. They'll tell him it will be a thirty-minute wait."

"Are you trying to get him as mad as possible, or throw him a party?" Noah shook his head, a smile curling the corner of his mouth.

"Hush. This is the part where you come in. You'll need to set up a generator in the pavilion, hook up a small fridge and some speakers."

"I can do that."

"Then I will suggest to him we go for a walk on the golf course while we wait. We'll have his friends waiting out there, music, and beers."

"Okay. I think he might actually like that."

Silvia set down her mug and gave a decisive nod. "Of course he will. I realized something about your dad the last few months. He never let himself have any fun before, when he was working at the shop."

"I think you might be right." He knew that feeling well.

"So I will give him some fun. Even if I have to trick him into it."

Next to him on the couch, Vanessa clasped his hand and gave it a squeeze.

"You're having fun, too," she told Silvia. "I can tell."

"I am." Silvia's expression brightened. "He listens better now. And then he goes home at the end of the day and leaves me in peace."

"I'm so happy for you two. How did you keep him away this afternoon?" Vanessa asked.

Silvia grinned at her, conspiratorial. "I was honest. I told him I wanted time with my son and his wonderful girlfriend, and he could come by later. I told him the dirt he tracks in from the golf course bothers me, which is also the truth."

She sniffed. "I have to make him take off his shoes at the door. And sometimes his pants."

"Silvia." Heat crawled up Noah's neck, into his face.

"What?" Silvia turned to Vanessa. "He's always so shy about this stuff."

A smile played over Vanessa's features. She was probably remembering last night, when they'd started out on the couch watching a movie, but ended up making love halfway through, with him kneeling between her thighs, and nope, this was not a good time to think about that, or he'd never stop blushing.

But he was not always so shy.

"He's getting better about communicating," Vanessa said, and patted his knee.

And he was. He told her every day he loved her. And he backed it up with actions, something easier for him to do. She

Chapter 20

would never scrape her car or fill her gas tank again if it was up to him.

Not because she couldn't do those things for herself. But because she let him take care of her.

God, she was good to him, too. She knew how to massage the tension from his shoulders after work, how to get him to open up in a conversation. She knew how to listen for what he wasn't always able to say, because she was good like that.

After their tea, Silvia embraced each of them at the door.

"The two of you are meant to be. I'm so happy for both of you," she said.

"Thank you." Vanessa hugged Silvia, and then it was his turn.

"Take good care of her," Silvia told him.

She made brief eye contact, and he read the underlying message. She'd asked him about marriage and grandchildren more than once the last few months. Soon, he'd have to explain to her that Vanessa had never wanted children and never would, and he was fine with that. But he was working on the marriage part.

"I will," he said.

"Well. It's Tu B'Av, the day of true love," Silvia said. "Go enjoy the afternoon. And hibiscus tea increases passion. Or so I've heard."

She gave them a tiny smile before shutting the door. He'd wondered why she'd insisted on serving hot tea in the middle of summer. Apparently, she'd had a plan.

Back in the car, Vanessa turned to him. Her face was bright with mischief, the sunlight glinting off her cat-eye glasses. She'd worn a denim mini skirt and a pink silk tank top today, probably just to torture him.

"So it's Tu B'Av," she said. "I didn't realize until Silvia

211

mentioned it. I was thinking …"

He swallowed, feeling his thoughts slip as she traced a finger up his thigh.

"Uh. What were you thinking?"

"I thought I wanted to wait until Valentine's Day to open my box. But I'm also very curious. You won't give me any clues about what the ring looks like."

He sat up straighter, trying to clear his head. The wooden puzzle box sat at home on his dresser, unopened but always visible, the centerpiece of the room. The ring inside was a vintage art deco style ruby, bracketed by diamonds.

"But today is another day of love," she went on. "So I think I should open it when I get home."

His breath froze in his chest. "Really? You're serious?"

"Yep. The instructions are still in your wallet, right?"

"Yes." His brain couldn't seem to catch up. He'd been sure it would take years for her to be ready. He was so caught up in his racing thoughts that it took a moment to realize she'd unbuckled her seatbelt.

She dove at him, reaching for his back pocket.

A startled laugh broke out of him. "What are you doing?"

"I'm getting a head start." Her hand wedged behind him, palming his ass on her way into his pocket.

"You don't have to … Just let me give it to you." He twisted under her, but she was persistent, clinging to him and digging into his pocket until she extracted his wallet with an exclamation of triumph.

"Got it." She fell back into the seat, holding her prize.

"Listen, there's a lot of stuff in there. Let me—"

But she'd already opened it, and her hands froze as the accordion of laminated photos unfolded from the wallet's interior.

"Yeah, so …" he said.

"Noah. You have a lot of pictures of me here. Like, an excessive amount."

"I know."

"Most people keep these in their phone."

"I like to look at them. When I'm at work." The flush was back, creeping up his neck and flooding his face with heat.

Her eyes flashed up to him. "Why are you embarrassed by this? I like it."

"You do?"

"Uh-huh. Oh, here are the instructions." She pulled out the business card he'd stowed, which detailed the steps to unlock the puzzle box. Carefully, she folded the photos back up, closed the wallet, and handed it to him.

"So when we get home, I'm going to open that box. I might still need your help, full disclosure."

"Of course." He felt breathless, dizzy with loving her.

"Then I'm going to put that ring on my finger. If you want to ask me to marry you, you can. But as far as I'm concerned, you already did. You do it every day."

"I'll do it again," he said quickly.

"Good. And after that, do you know what we're going to do?"

"What?"

She looked up at him, eyes shining. "Whatever makes us happy. I'm sure we'll think of something."

He could think of a lot of things. But it didn't matter what else happened today, because she'd chosen him. He'd get to have this life with her. He shook his head, because somehow he'd made this happen. They'd made it happen together.

"Noah? Are you going to start the car?"

"Yeah." He cleared his throat. "Let's go get engaged."

Afterword

I continue to be amazed that I'm writing books and publishing them. What a privilege, and it's so much fun, too! The process of writing books has uncovered layers in me I didn't know existed—layers of determination, creativity, and heart.

First off, I want to thank all the readers of my books. Thank you for taking the time to pick up my book and give it a shot. Reading indie authors, talking about our books to friends, leaving reviews—all of these things enable writers to keep doing what we do! For that, I am so incredibly grateful.

Thank you to my wonderful, supportive family, who have read my books and cheered me on. I couldn't do it without you.

To my beta readers, Rebecca and Jessica, thank you for pointing out so many things which have made my books immeasurably stronger, every time. Your second set of eyes are invaluable to me, always.

To my sensitivity readers, Annie and Rachel, thank you for looking at my books through different lenses. Every word of feedback has been helpful beyond measure.

To my online writing groups, particularly the Baguettes,

thank you for your unending kindness, help, and support. I'm really not sure I could do this without writing pals to laugh and cry with.

To the indie author community, my endless thanks for making this all seem possible, when it was so intimidating at first. I mean, it's still intimidating, but I understand the process much better now.

Lastly, to you. Thank you for reading this book. When an author writes, and a reader reads, we're connected in a shared experience of the story. And I think that's pretty special.

About the Author

S.M. Levine grew up with her face in a book, and now she writes steamy, emotional contemporary romance about imperfect people who find true love. She lives in the Midwest with her family and a small assortment of cats.

You can connect with me on:
- 🌐 https://www.smlevineauthor.com
- 🔗 https://www.instagram.com/sm_levine
- 🔗 https://bsky.app/profile/smlevine.bsky.social

Subscribe to my newsletter:
- ✉ https://www.smlevineauthor.com

Also by S.M. Levine

Check out these other titles in The Well Space series!

The Well Space Series:

Less than Perfect

Trial Run

Couples Session

Over Work (coming fall 2025)